"Mister, you ain't seen nothing yet."

Tyler's jaw tightened. She just wouldn't let up. That lazy drawl of hers pushed him over the razor's edge. "So when do you want to start interviewing me?" he asked.

"Right now."

No more thinking. Instead, he'd just show her. His hands gripping her shoulders, he pulled her against him and lowered his head. The moment his mouth covered hers, he knew he was in trouble. The lady tasted like the sweetest of sins and the most decadent of delights. And she kissed him back with equal enthusiasm.

"Damn you, Countess. The first minute I saw you I knew you were trouble. So go ahead, take your best shot. That's what you're looking to do, isn't it?"

Tyler braced himself for the first blow. Instead, her arms flew languidly around his neck and she pulled his face back down to hers.

"Fasten your seat belt, cowboy," she murmured, "you're in for the kind of ride no wild bronco could give you."

ABOUT THE AUTHOR

Linda Randall Wisdom is well-known to romance readers. She writes all kinds of stories, but has always had a weakness for Westerns. "After my first John Wayne movie," she says, "I was hooked for life." When she saw the film *McLintock!* at age eleven, Linda went home and wrote it from memory. These days she gets more creative, and draws inspiration from her husband, two dogs and a houseful of exotic birds in Southern California.

Books by Linda Randall Wisdom

HARLEQUIN AMERICAN ROMANCE

Don't miss any of our special offers. Write to us at the following address for information on our newest releases.

Harlequin Reader Service
P.O. Box 1397, Buffalo, NY 14240
Canadian address: P.O. Box 603,
Fort Erie, Ont. L2A 5X3

LINDA RANDALL WISDOM

THE COUNTESS AND THE COWBOY

Harlequin Books

TORONTO • NEW YORK • LONDON
AMSTERDAM • PARIS • SYDNEY • HAMBURG
STOCKHOLM • ATHENS • TOKYO • MILAN
MADRID • WARSAW • BUDAPEST • AUCKLAND

Published May 1993

ISBN 0-373-16487-4

THE COUNTESS AND THE COWBOY

Prologue

"*Cara,* have pity." His handsome liquid brown eyes and smooth Italian accent begged for understanding, but there was little hope of a reprieve. She was beautiful, but her furious aqua eyes told him not to expect such a thing until hell froze over.

"Me, have pity? After what you did to me? Giancarlo, I should shoot you where you sit, you slimy snake, you sneaky underhanded worm, you conniving son of a..." She used both hands to brace the deadly looking revolver she aimed at him.

"Letitia, you're attracting attention." Giancarlo's gaze darted worriedly from right to left. He lowered his cultured voice to a confidential level. It began to show more than a hint of strain. But then, any man would feel some anxiety if he had a woman pointing a gun directly at his heart.

Letitia kept her eyes on the perspiring man seated at a café table on the shady patio. She was so focused on him, it was easy to ignore the mildly curious onlookers who had just walked off the golf course or the tennis courts in search of a cold drink. While the Southern California elite knew enough not to display vulgar interest in a woman standing on the clubhouse patio aiming a gun at one of the guests, many couldn't help but wonder who the pair was. When they joined the exclusive Bel Air club they had no idea such excitement was included in the dues.

In the back of her mind, Letitia DeMarco realized this little incident would probably result in her guest privileges being revoked. Good thing such possibilities didn't upset her. Right now, she had more pressing matters to resolve. Mainly, Giancarlo.

"And to think I was almost fool enough to marry you," she snapped. "Tell me, Giancarlo, how many people have you duped over the years since your less than glorious retreat from Italy? Does anyone else know your family disinherited you because of a similar scandal with one of their friend's daughters? That they insisted you even drop your family name because they're so ashamed of you? Let me see."

She tapped her forefinger against her lips in exaggerated thought. Her one hand held the revolver with a steady grip. "Didn't it have something to do with getting your brother's fiancée pregnant and then refusing to do the honorable thing by marrying her? Instead, you accepted a healthy settlement to stay away. And since then, you've proposed to dozens of women, as long as they're wealthy, of course. You'd get what money you could from them and take off for greener pastures. You have quite a little con game going on, don't you?"

Giancarlo Reynaldo, a.k.a. too many names to count, began to sweat under Letitia's deadly aim. The young woman he'd been romancing had fled the moment Letitia marched outside with the gun leveled at him. Letitia had smiled at the woman and suggested she might want to leave. She didn't waste any time running into the bar screaming there was a crazy woman out there with her fiancé and someone should call the police. The club executives being the types who disliked any kind of publicity, much less the negative kind, opted to alert their private security staff to the problem on the patio. They all were familiar with Letitia DeMarco, whom they considered a very lovely and very reasonable woman.

Letitia hadn't stopped to think this could be a bad idea or that she could even end up in jail for threatening a man with a gun. She only knew the man cowering in front of her, the man she'd thought she wanted to marry, turned out to be the worst kind of man a woman could have the misfortune to hook up with.

Giancarlo managed a smile and slowly stood up with his arms wide open as if to embrace her. "*Cara,* let's go somewhere and discuss this," he crooned. "You know I would never do anything to hurt you. I love you." He took a step forward.

"Stop right there!" Letitia lowered the barrel. "You take one more step and I will shoot off what you hold so valuable."

His eyes widened in alarm as he realized she was aiming at his crotch. "Letitia, you would not do such a horrible thing."

"Watch me." Her deep aqua eyes narrowed in concentration. She could hear voices murmuring in the background and realized her time was limited. "You owe me one hundred and fifty thousand dollars and I want it now."

"If there is a problem we can meet at my bank tomorrow and I will do all I can to help you."

Her laughter held no humor. "Which bank, Giancarlo? The one you *claim* to have an account at or the one that states your balance is twenty-three dollars and forty-six cents?" She dropped the bomb with ladylike aplomb. "I had a fascinating talk with your father last evening. He is very unhappy with you, Giancarlo. So unhappy that he isn't going to send you this quarter's check."

Giancarlo's face turned a sickly gray as he listened to his true past thrown out to the rapidly growing audience. Then his handsome features just as quickly turned sharp. As a man who lived by his wits and charm, he could see which would work with Letitia.

"What do you want?"

Letitia smiled. "My money."

"I don't have it and you seem to already know that," he snapped.

She nodded her agreement. "You probably spent it on your next victim. But that won't get you off the hook, Giancarlo. I did some checking and you do have some property. A cattle ranch in Montana. All you have to do is sign this transfer of ownership and we'll be even." She reached inside her jacket pocket and pulled out a sheet of paper. "I'm sure Lawrence, over there, will be only too happy to witness it for us. Won't you, dear?" She flashed a brilliant smile at a silver-haired man standing off to one side. Lawrence's answering smile was feeble. "I assume he'll agree to help just to get me off the property within the next five minutes."

"The property is worth much more than a hundred and fifty thousand dollars!" Giancarlo argued.

Her glorious eyes spat fire. "Either pay me the money or sign over the ranch. Those are your choices.

Unless you'd rather I call in the authorities. The first
charge will be fraud, then all the others will fall neatly
into place. I wonder how many victims I might be able
to find who'd be delighted to testify against you."

Giancarlo looked around for any semblance of
support. Each person he silently sought discreetly
turned away.

"All right, give me the paper," he growled, snatching it out of her hand. He didn't bother to read it but
merely scrawled his name by a red x.

"It also states if you step foot on the Montana
property you will be shot on sight," she advised, using the gun to wave Lawrence over. "We just need two
witnesses. Howard, would you mind?"

"Letitia, I never thought you were the type to make
such a horrible scene," one bikini-clad brunette murmured from the sidelines. "There are other ways to
handle such an impropriety."

"Those ways take too long and the victim never
wins, Buffy," she stated, stepping forward and keeping one eye on Giancarlo as she signed her name on the
dotted line.

"This isn't legal," Giancarlo argued, trying one last
time.

"Oh, it's very legal. I made sure of that," she assured him. "I had a very good lawyer draw up these
papers. You just sold me your ranch and I have plenty
of witnesses to attest to that." Her voice softened.
"Face it, darling, you've lost your entrée here. After
today, invitations to parties will suddenly disappear,
your calls won't be taken, you won't get a decent res-
ervation at the 'right' restaurants and people will suddenly develop amnesia when they see you on the street.
I suggest you look for new territory."

"Mrs. DeMarco, may I have the gun please?" One of the club's security officers approached her with caution when he thought she seemed more composed.

She turned to hand it to him.

"It's probably empty anyway," Giancarlo sneered, finding his courage now that he felt her power was taken away from her. He lifted his drink to his lips.

Letitia spun around with the gun still in her hand. The loud report assaulted the viewers' ears just as Giancarlo's glass shattered in his hand, the liquid streaming down his silk-covered arm. His curse could have been a prayer as he stared wild-eyed at her.

"Mother's second husband believed women should shoot as well as men," she explained, handing the gun to the stunned security man, whose lips twitched with amusement and respect at a woman who knew how to make her point.

Letitia scanned the document and carefully tucked it in her purse. She flashed her winning smile at the onlookers who appeared as shocked as Giancarlo.

"I really hate to shoot and run," she told them. "You see, it's just this little quirk I have. I hate to be cheated and he was going to pay one way or another. Although, I am glad I didn't have to shoot him. Blood is so difficult to get out of silk." She spared Giancarlo a quick glance as she was escorted out of the patio area with a security guard on each side. "Have a nice day."

"THAT SON OF A BITCH!" Tyler slapped the letter with the attorney's letterhead against his gloved palm.

"You seem a little upset, boy," J.T. drawled, taking the paper out of his hand and reading it. "So he sold it."

"He promised I would have first chance if he decided to sell," he growled, prowling the empty corral like a jungle cat who'd been caged. "And now he's sold it to a woman! Some flighty Italian socialite who probably doesn't know a damn thing about ranching or how I've had to run this place on a shoestring because he never came through with the funds we need so badly to keep this place going."

"Maybe she'll have the money to do what's necessary. As for her not knowing anything, if she doesn't, show her."

The older man's quiet suggestion brought him up short. "I will *not* work for a woman."

J.T. searched his pockets and brought out a pack of cigarettes, which Tyler immediately confiscated.

"You're not supposed to have these," he scolded. "Besides, we have a problem here."

"*You* have the problem."

"I can see her now," Tyler grumbled. "Dark hair, brown eyes, sounding like someone in one of those foreign films, wears silk and lace. She'll take one look at this place and head back to Italy."

"This lawyer's office is in California," J.T. commented, looking at the letter.

"I don't give a damn where she goes back to, as long as she goes." Tyler's gray eyes turned cold. "Giancarlo was happy to keep his distance, although some contact would have been nice all the times I wrote to him about our problems. This place could be turned into a paying proposition if we just had the funds." Frustration laced his voice.

J.T., who'd been ranch foreman until his retirement when Tyler took over, understood the younger man's frustration. "Then charm the money out of the lady," he joked.

Tyler looked at the letter again. "She's due to arrive next week." He looked off into the distance. "Some damn Italian countess. I give her less than twenty-four hours."

J.T.'s eyes lit up. Minor gambling on the property was one of the men's favorite pastimes. "Sounds like the beginning of a pool here." He rubbed his hands with glee.

"Put me down for two hours," Tyler said grimly, before striding toward the rear part of the main house. "I guess I better give Myrna the bad news. I just hope she doesn't fly off the handle and burn dinner."

J.T. was on his way to the bunkhouse. "Guess I better start drawing up the pool. Once the other men hear, bets will go wild. Somebody is going to be making a lot of money on this."

"An Italian countess," Tyler groused. "Terrific."

Chapter One

"I want him dead, Jack. I want the man drawn and quartered and cut into tiny pieces and fed to those horrible bats you have in the belfry. No, that's not all I want! That's only the beginning of his torture. I want Stephano to suffer for what he did to me!" Her hands gestured with the same fury she used for words.

She was so engrossed in her dire threats she was unaware of the man in the doorway watching her with grim eyes. She was standing by the makeshift metal counter that served as an airline reservations desk, a shipping desk for UPS and a Sears catalog order desk.

Tyler Barnes gazed at the woman with eyes that were bleary from sitting up half the night with a colicky horse and having to get up a few hours early to make the trip out here. To have to drive two hours to pick up the new owner wasn't on his list of important things to do for the day. To discover the lady with the Italian last name was very much American with a nasty temper and bloodthirsty nature was quite a surprise. Ironically, a nice surprise since she also turned out to be beautiful.

Tyler leaned against the wall with his arms crossed in front of his chest. He had an idea that the show was only beginning and he didn't intend to miss one moment.

"Of course, I know he's dead! That has nothing to do with it, Jack. Well, yes, it does, because I want Stephano's body exhumed. I don't believe he died," she went on, unperturbed that everyone in the tiny Quonset hut was unabashedly eavesdropping on this exotic creature's tirade. It was proving much more interesting than any gossip that had filtered through there in the last month. "His family probably put him up to this and he's hiding somewhere, so he wouldn't have to continue paying my alimony. Jack, they canceled all my credit cards! Do you know what it feels like to watch some grinning idiot cut up your American Express card? It is not a pretty sight! As for Giancarlo..." As if the English language wasn't enough, she suddenly lapsed into Italian, the words sounding like angry music as she gestured with her free hand.

"Wow, she even knows a foreign language," an awestruck adolescent standing near Tyler breathed as he stared at Letitia. "Whaddya think she's saying?"

Tyler was too busy concentrating on the lady's legs. They were visible under a white silk skirt that still looked fresh as a daisy considering the dirt that flew around the tiny airfield. How did she do it?

"She's probably talking about more ways of torturing the men in her life. Something tells me what she's saying isn't fit for mixed company," he replied, straightening up and walking toward her. "Guess I better get the lady off the phone."

"Jack, I know you can do this. You must know a lot of people. Call someone in the mob. If anyone can find Stephano, they can," she insisted, so engrossed in her tirade she didn't notice that a tall man dressed in dusty jeans and shirt with a sweat-stained Stetson perched on top of his head now stood next to her.

"Ticia, calm down, you're going overboard again," a man's voice could be heard clearly as Tyler plucked the receiver out of her hand.

Letitia looked up and up until she met a pair of steel gray eyes. "What do you think you're doing?" Curiosity instead of anger colored her voice.

"The countess here will have to call you back," he told the man on the line. "Have a nice day." He carefully replaced the receiver in the cradle.

Letitia still didn't look the least bit upset that her call was so abruptly terminated. Not when she was so curious about the man who'd so neatly cut Jack off.

"You just hung up on my brother," she informed Tyler.

"If he's your brother, he'll understand why." Tyler looked at the pile of luggage surrounding her. "This all yours?"

She nodded, still studying him in a manner that would disconcert most men. Except Tyler Barnes wasn't most men.

Tyler bent down and picked up the nearest cases. He sighed as he viewed the remaining cases, especially the one that looked suspiciously like an animal carrier.

She probably brought one of those yappy poodles with her, he thought wearily, hearing tiny sounds emit from the interior. Duffy'll turn him into mincemeat inside of five minutes.

"Think you'll have enough clothes?" he asked mildly, heading outside without bothering to see if she was following him. "Will the main part of your wardrobe be arriving by moving van?"

"I'm never sure what to wear, so I brought a little of everything," she replied, unperturbed by his testy manner. She negotiated the rocky ground in three-inch white leather high heels with an ease that amazed Tyler, who fully expected her to trip and fall on her white silk butt. She looked around with genuine interest. "This is so amazing. I've never been to this part of the country before. Are you really a cowboy?"

"I'm your foreman," he explained with a patience he didn't feel inside. The worst part was there was something else brewing deep inside him as he darted quick looks at the lovely woman standing nearby. Lord, he'd never seen anyone so beautiful in his life, outside of magazines. She smelled like heaven and looked like the star from a man's fantasy. He'd be surprised if she lasted more than an hour in this country.

"Oh, do I call you foreman or do you have a name?" She skidded to a stop next to a dusty blue pickup truck. Tyler tossed the luggage into the truck bed without regard to the expensive leather. Letitia tried not to wince at the obvious damage to her Louis Vuitton cases. Even those nasty baggage handlers in Nice hadn't been this violent.

"Tyler Barnes." He turned on his heel and walked back into the hut for the last of the cases.

"Are you always so talkative?"

He stared back. "Well ma'am, out here if there's nothin' important to say, we just don't say anything."

She mulled over his words. "That makes sense." She gazed toward the truck's passenger door. "This is all so new to me that I'm not sure how to act."

"Yeah, we figured that." He couldn't keep his eyes off her white silk skirt and soft aqua blouse that matched her eyes.

Letitia followed the direction of his eyes. "I guess I'm a bit overdressed." She wrinkled her nose. "I didn't think the airport here would be, well, like this." She looked around at the expanse of dirt and tall weeds decorating the exterior of the World War II vintage Quonset hut set squarely in the middle. "Or that the pilot of the plane would look like someone out of a horror film. And believe me, if anyone knows about horror, it's me..." Her words trailed off while she stared at her foreman's back as he headed back to the building.

"What the hell is in this thing?" Tyler roared a few minutes later, walking out of the Quonset holding the animal carrier as far from his body as his arm could reach while the occupant yowled shrilly enough to break glass.

"Oh, my baby!" Letitia headed straight for the carrier. "Sweetheart, I know you're upset, but it wouldn't be a good idea to let you out now," she crooned through the wire door. "You'll be out of the carrier and safe in your new home very soon."

Tyler scowled. "What is it?"

"*He* is my cat, Le Chat," she explained, taking the carrier from him. "He's very upset because he hates to travel. I know he would have preferred to stay behind in Salem, but Jack said he's positive Le Chat would be happier with me than with him. He only says that because he hates him," she confided.

Tyler looked upward, appealing to a much higher power who, he was convinced, was playing a very nasty trick on him. "Then I hope *he* is a good mouser because that's the only use we have for cats around here."

Letitia looked horrified at his pronouncement. "Le Chat is not a mouser. He has an impeccable bloodline."

Tyler took the carrier from her and set it in the back of the truck. "Well, countess, out here, bloodlines don't mean much except with horses and cattle." He herded Letitia to the passenger door of the truck with the same ease he herded cattle. He planted his hand against her rear end and unceremoniously pushed her onto the seat.

"I could have gotten in here myself!" she protested, looking down at him.

"Not in that skirt." He walked around the front of the truck to the driver's side.

Tyler swung his body behind the steering wheel and started the engine. He swore under his breath when the cat's yowling protest vibrated through the air.

"He doesn't like riding in the back," Letitia told him.

"He'll get used to it," he clipped, steering the truck down the pothole-infested drive.

"He also holds grudges and he knows you were the one who put him back there." She shifted her body into a more comfortable position—not all that easy on a seat that was patched with duct tape. "Le Chat always gets even."

"I'll survive." He shifted gears, wishing she'd quit wiggling because every movement sent a wave of sexy perfume his way. Damn, why did she have to be one of the most beautiful women he's ever seen? Why couldn't she look like one of those horse-faced toothy society matrons he'd seen in old movies on TV, instead of having lovely delicate features with sparkling eyes and a warm smile? Yet she dressed and looked like old money. Silk clothing, expensive leather shoes, hair pulled up in an elaborate braid with a ribbon running through it the same color as her blouse. No woman should look that good! He wondered how long it would take before she begged to go back to civilization. He wished he could remember what the odds were in the betting pool. Everyone had chipped in five bucks; he'd given her two hours. He now shortened his estimate to half that time. Besides, he reminded himself, just because she's lovely on the outside doesn't mean she's all that lovely inside. Still, if she has the money necessary to sink into the ranch he won't complain. He tried to tune out her voice as she chattered away, but it was easier said than done.

"It's very remote, isn't it?" Letitia chattered as she looked right and left. "I mean, there's so much empty land around. I'm surprised real estate developers haven't come out this way."

She hoped she didn't sound like some flighty socialite to Tyler and feared that was exactly what she sounded like. She hadn't expected her ranch foreman to look like he stepped out of one of those old cigarette ads. She expected him to be gray-haired, paunchy and chewing tobacco. Maybe even be unshaven. Instead, he turned out to be tall and very good-looking. Seated this close to him, she could inhale the warm aroma of horse mixed with male sweat. Her eyes lingered on his hands resting on the steering wheel. She'd bet there were calluses on the fingertips and in the palm and they'd feel raspy against her bare skin. She almost shook her head in denial. Where did that mental picture come from? She wasn't here to find a man. Not with her lousy track record where the opposite sex was involved. She noted a pale blue and purple bruise on his thumb that spread across his nail. She winced at the idea of what kind of pounding could have caused something that must have hurt like hell when it happened. She had to bring herself sharply back to the here and now to catch Tyler's answer to her spoken question.

"As you said, it's too remote, although most of this land is either privately owned or owned by the government and we lease grazing rights. Besides, no big-city yuppie wants this kind of commute, much less live so far from the symphony, the theater, Rodeo Drive," he tacked on in a sardonic tone. "Although, we do seem to be getting movie stars out here because they want the privacy."

She tipped her head to one side, looking at him with eyes he thought saw more than he wanted to show. He was beginning to fear this lady might not be the fluff ball she'd first appeared.

"Opera puts me to sleep," she stated. "Now, tell me about the ranch."

"We run cattle."

Her face brightened. "Oh, like in the movies with cattle drives and stampedes and all?"

"Stampedes aren't exactly a pastime we encourage. It tends to upset the cattle," Tyler gritted, swiftly changing his estimation of her, again.

His hands tightened on the steering wheel. Damn! Why did she have to have seduced Giancarlo into signing the ranch over to her? Giancarlo had practically promised Tyler he could buy it from him. Giancarlo had never been interested in being a hands-on owner. In order for the ranch to pull out of its slump and have a chance to succeed, it really needed the personal touch. And Tyler, with his love for the land, knew he could give it just that. He still had a chance, his inner voice intruded. The lady looked as if ranch life wouldn't agree with silk clothing and fancy hairstyles, so maybe he could strike a deal with her.

"We'll be on your land in about half an hour," he announced suddenly. He mentally cursed the moment he spoke because Letitia's attention was now focused on him and with each movement of her body the haunting fragrance of her perfume floated in his direction.

"And then how much longer before we reach the house?"

"Another hour and a half or so."

Letitia leaned forward and peered through the windshield. "The ranch is that big?" Her hushed voice was filled with awe.

"You need a lot of land with cattle," he said, frowning. "Tell me something, countess, exactly how much do you know about ranches?"

"They either have cattle, sheep or horses, cowboys work on them and—" her brow wrinkled in thought "—and the old men chew tobacco, which sounds positively disgusting."

"Where exactly did you grow up?" Tyler demanded. He couldn't believe it. What she said should have come out sounding stupid, but instead, she merely sounded like someone who just didn't know.

Letitia crossed her ankles in perfect finishing-school fashion. The soft sound of silk sliding against perfumed silk was loud in Tyler's ears.

"I'd have to say most of my schooling was in England, although I did spend a year in Switzerland and another in Florence," she explained. "My mother loves to travel any chance she can get and my brother and I usually ended up in school wherever we happened to be at the time. She preferred England because she felt they offered the best schooling. Although the uniforms we were forced to wear were hideous. When I complained about them, I was told they would build character. That isn't how I saw it."

"I thought you were Italian," he commented.

Letitia shook her head. "No, born American, schooled European," she replied. "Mother left Connecticut years ago after she married Jack's father. She met mine in Berlin. He was with the American embassy there. Her present husband has something to do with British politics."

He was beginning to doubt that anything she said would surprise him. "Your mother had three husbands?"

"Actually, she's had five. Jack's father died of a heart attack, mine divorced her in favor of a cabaret singer and she went on to marry three more times. Her third husband died and she threw her fourth one out when she found out he had a mistress. She met her present husband two years ago. Luckily, she and Percival have been very happy." She wrinkled her nose. "Can you honestly imagine anyone named Percival? And he's not the type of man you can call Percy, either."

Her laughter washed over Tyler like warm rain. He hunched his shoulders as if the action would just banish her aura from him. He should have known better. The lady seemed to stick to him like glue. The sooner they reached the ranch house and she was inside, the happier he'd be. He deliberately tuned her out as he concentrated on navigating the twisting rocky road.

Except the speed only accomplished one thing, keeping Letitia unbalanced on the lumpy seat with her body bouncing right and left, usually left against Tyler. And Le Chat's angry yowls threatened to shatter his eardrums.

"Sorry," she murmured, after bumping into him the fourth time.

He gritted his teeth. "No problem." Oh sure, no problem. The lady smelled better than anything he'd ever smelled in his entire life and the source of that smell probably cost more than he made in a year! Does her bare skin feel as soft and silky as her clothing? What would she feel like in bed? He damned himself for even thinking it. Didn't he have enough problems without thinking of sliding her into his bed?

"I don't think Le Chat is having a good ride."

"Cats can endure anything."

"Yes, but Le Chat isn't just a cat. He has a pedigree longer than most humans. One of his ancestors was with Catherine De Medici."

"Well, hell, maybe we should have brought the limousine," Tyler muttered, pulling the wheel hard to the right to avoid a particularly nasty pothole.

"Considering the state of this road, it probably wouldn't have been a good idea. I guess it would cost too much to pave the road, wouldn't it?" Letitia rashly commented before she noted Tyler's dark frown.

"Yep."

Her face lit up. "You really do say yep! I thought that was only in the movies and in books."

Tyler heaved a sigh. "Countess, there's a lot of things we say around here, most of them not fit for a lady."

"You'd be surprised what I've heard over the years between my brother, his friends and later on with my ex-husband." Her lovely features darkened. "The louse."

"Hey, if he's not paying you enough alimony you can always take him back to court for more," Tyler suggested.

"I would do more than that if he hadn't decided to die on me when his polo pony fell on him. I'm just glad the horse wasn't hurt. No, Stephano deserved a much nastier death," she murmured. "And I would have been only too happy to arrange one for him."

"So because of your husband, uh, ex-husband, you're a countess?"

She slanted a look at Tyler. "No, you're the one who granted me that title. Stephano's family are only minor royalty. Very minor. Besides, I've been called much worse over the years."

"So how'd you meet Giancarlo?" Tyler asked.

"At a party in Los Angeles. I should have known he was a complete bastard. He was much too charming. Stephano had been charming. At first. Then polo became his first love." She raised her hands, palms up in a and-that-was-that gesture.

"I'm just wonderin' how you ended up with the ranch." He figured he'd learn all he could as long as she was going to speak so openly.

"Giancarlo owed me a lot of money and he preferred signing the ranch over to going to jail," she explained. "If I'd had my way he would have . . ."

"Been drawn and quartered among other things," Tyler finished for her.

She grimaced. "I guess I went a little overboard on the phone. Luckily, Jack understands my temper. He doesn't have one. The man is so cool and composed it's downright scary. It must have something to do with the books he writes."

He didn't want to ask. He wanted to avoid chitchat altogether. Still, he had to find out. "Your brother writes books?"

Letitia nodded. "Horror. Have you ever read anything by Jack Montgomery?"

Tyler was now impressed. "The man who wrote *Black Moon?* It was very good. One of the men read it and had trouble sleeping for a week. The book jacket said he's written a lot of books, but I'd never seen them before."

Letitia nodded in agreement. "He's only been published in Europe until recently. He moved to Salem, Massachusetts a little over a year ago and got married just after the first of the year. Talk about the perfect life-style. He's living in a house haunted by a man who hung himself at the turn of the century, his wife is a witch's descendant and her children believe in magic so much they cast a spell to conjure up a father. It's the Addams Family without Thing and Lurch, but they do have a housekeeper who had to have been one of the witches in *Macbeth.*"

Tyler shook his head. "Great, the countess and her whole family are loony tunes," he muttered, glancing out the side window. Landmarks told him the ride would only be another ten minutes. Ten minutes that would seem like a lifetime.

Letitia wasn't sure which was worse: Le Chat's agitated yowling in the back of the truck or Tyler's glares. She subdued a sigh. During her flight here she went over in her mind how she was going to handle this. She had vowed to let this be the beginning of a new life for herself. A life that would give her complete independence. How good that word sounded! After all these years of having to first rely on her mother then Stephano and even her brother, she felt she was well and truly on her own now and vowed to make this new venture work. After all, with ranch hands doing all the heavy work, how hard could it be to run a ranch? And her foreman was supposed to oversee everything, wasn't he? She straightened her shoulders, feeling more confident about her future than she had in a long while.

Her foreman. He was dusty from the long drive to town. His craggy face was bristling with a heavy beard, features that looked grim enough to belong on a statue. Eyes that beautiful shade of gray shouldn't be so cold and condemning, she decided. The man was clearly not too happy to have her here. Well, too bad, she was here and intending to stay whether he liked it or not!

Letitia was so lost in her thoughts she didn't realize the truck was slowing to a stop until Tyler spoke.

"Well, countess, welcome to Running Springs Ranch." Faint sarcasm coated his words. "Hope it's all you thought you would be."

Letitia's expectant smile faltered then died completely as she looked past Tyler's impressive chest toward a sprawling clapboard house with discolored peeling gray paint that left the exterior looking like it had been left untended for many a season. It was a toss-up whether the roof or the weathered porch would collapse first.

"And I thought Jack's house was the ultimate in horror," she murmured, before looking up at Tyler's chiseled profile and asking a tad hopefully, "Is this the bunkhouse?"

He turned to face her with a sardonic smile pasted on his lips. "No, countess, this is the main house where the *owner* resides, although I guess it doesn't look anything like the castles and mansions you're used to." He confirmed her worst fears. "I admit it might need a little work, but I'm sure you can spruce it up thanks to all that money you got from your titled ex-husband before he kicked the bucket or got crushed by his horse or whatever he did."

"Money? I don't have *any* money! His family canceled my credit cards the day of Stephano's funeral!" she blurted out, going nose to nose with him. With her hands braced on her hips, her chest was pushed out until it brushed against his shirt front. "All I have to my name is this ranch!"

Tyler's mouth dropped open in shock. He could only stare at her, unable to believe what he just heard. He not only got saddled with a fancy dancy countess, but a broke one at that!

Chapter Two

Tyler stared up at the sky as if a higher power might suddenly speak up and assure him this was all a horrible nightmare he would soon wake up from. At the very least, a very nasty joke. Neither happened.

"I don't believe this," he muttered, slowly shaking his head. He stared down at the ground looking for that same answer. His anger sliced through her like a hot knife. "You're dressed in clothing that probably costs more than I make in a year, you were married to some high mucky muck Italian member of royalty, and you don't have a cent?" By the time he finished, his voice was a low roar.

Letitia was unperturbed by his fury. She prided herself on remaining calm in the most upsetting situations. Right now, she felt this was a true test of her ability. "I don't know why you're so worried. I'm not destitute. I have the ranch." She looked a bit doubtful as she gazed at the house. "Of course, it does need a little work," she murmured under her breath.

Tyler kept shaking his head as he walked around to the rear of the truck and lowered the tailgate with a measured bang.

"Ben, get over here and help me get this un-
loaded," he barked at a young man who stood near
the barn watching them with open curiosity. "Starting with *this*." He picked up the animal carrier and
handed it to the younger man as he walked up. Ben
winced at the earsplitting sounds coming from the interior.

"My poor baby!" Letitia reached for the carrier. At
the same time the latch loosened and the cat flew out
of the interior like a tawny blond haze. "Le Chat!"

"Duffy!" Tyler yelled at the same time as a black
shepherd-wolf mix appeared from a corner of the
house. The moment the large canine saw a member of
his worst enemy, he chased after it. The cat promptly
raced for a straggly tree near the house.

"Le Chat, you don't know how to climb a tree!"
Letitia wailed, racing after the terrified feline.

"Duffy, get back here!" Tyler ordered the barking
dog who was hot on the cat's heels. Pretty soon, Le
Chat was cowering on a branch well above the dog's
head as he leapt upward, barking madly at his prey.

"He's going to kill my cat!" Letitia appealed to
Tyler, grasping his shirtsleeve. "Please, don't let it
happen!"

"Lady, don't give me any ideas." His grim expression ordered her to remain silent as he grabbed hold of
the dog's collar and got him under control. It took all
of his strength to drag the lunging dog back.

Letitia looked up at the cat who now mewed pit-
eously from his perch. She couldn't remember ever
seeing him looking so upset. "Someone has to get him
down. He doesn't know anything about tree climbing."

"He got up there, he can figure out how to get down." He handed the excited dog over to Ben and strode toward the house with a ground-eating stride.

Letitia looked from her cat who looked thoroughly miserable to Tyler who now looked murderous. "I want my cat down. Now."

"Then get him down yourself." He walked back to the truck and picked up a couple of her suitcases, tossing them onto the porch.

Letitia marched after him intent on giving him a piece of her mind. "You are the most inconsiderate, idiotic..." She ran up the steps, hot on his heels as she ticked off the insults.

"Ma'am, that third step..." Ben's warning was almost too late.

Luckily Tyler turned as Letitia started up the steps and caught her just as one heel started to crash through the fragile wood. She looked up startled by his firm grip on her arm and aware of the many sensations racing through her body—the heat of his skin against hers, the faint not unpleasant scent of horse, sweat and man and the way his gray eyes bored through hers, the irises widening just a fraction. The man was not entirely immune to her! And he didn't like it, either. She carefully schooled her features so he wouldn't know she felt that electric jolt too. And that was just from his touch. What would happen if that firm line of a mouth covered hers? Tasted her skin? Nuzzled her neck? She swiftly brought herself back to sanity.

"Thank you," she murmured, forcing herself to continue looking into his eyes. The steel had turned a bit softer, not much, but many would consider it *something*.

"No problem. It wouldn't do to have the new owner fall and break her neck her first day here," he said huskily, releasing her arm.

She was stung. "Yes, I guess it wouldn't look good for the foreman's reputation. Not unless he was able to push her first."

"Countess, don't give me any ideas." He pulled open the screen door with more force than necessary.

"And don't call me count—" Letitia glared at his retreating back as he entered the house without bothering to hold the door open for her, "—ess." She raised her chin in a gesture her brother would have taken to mean Head for the hills. Letitia's on the warpath. She snatched the screen door handle and flung it open, marching inside with all the pomp and circumstance Tyler would expect. She skidded to a stop at the sight before her. Her eyes widened in shock.

"What happened here?"

Tyler grinned. It was nice to see *her* stunned after the surprises he'd had in the past couple of hours. "A woman hasn't lived in this house for more than twenty years and maid service out here is almost nonexistent."

Letitia entered what she supposed to be the living room although with the dirt and dust covering every surface of furniture and hardwood floors, it wasn't easy to tell. As far as she was concerned, she couldn't imagine a woman had *ever* lived here since the furniture was scarred from bootheels and what looked suspiciously like gouges from spurs on the coffee table. She walked over to the table and picked up a newspaper, holding it gingerly between her fingertips. She grimaced when she read the date.

"Obviously no one has cleaned in here since June seventh, nineteen seventy-eight." She dropped the paper back onto the table.

"Your old buddy, Giancarlo, was an absentee owner and Harvey, who owned the place before him, preferred the bunkhouse," Tyler explained. "Don't worry, I'm sure with some elbow grease you'll have this place spit-shined in no time." He walked back outside and carried in more of her luggage.

Letitia winced when she heard Le Chat's continued frantic yowling outside. "You have to get him down," she insisted.

"He's a cat. He knows how to get down."

Her eyes blazed brilliant color. "*Now,* please."

Tyler's jaw tightened. "Yes ma'am, anything you say ma'am." He swept his hat in front of him in a mocking bow before he sauntered outside with Letitia right behind him. He took his sweet time strolling toward the tree.

"You'll be fine soon, sweetheart," she crooned to her cat, who now clung to one of the highest branches while looking wildly around for help.

Tyler sighed as he handed his hat to Letitia and rolled up his sleeves. "This is ridiculous," he muttered, reaching up and grabbing hold of the lowest branch and swinging himself up. He glanced down and cursed at the sight of several of the men walking over to see what was going on.

"Ma'am, it would be better if we just let the cat come down on his own," Ben ventured. "Cats are real strange critters. They don't like you telling them what to do. And when they're scared, they get pretty nasty."

"Le Chat has a very loving nature," Letitia frostily informed him. "He wouldn't harm anyone."

"Ow! Damn you, cat!" Tyler's language grew more colorful as he sucked his wounded hand. The men's laughter subsided under his dark glare. Finally, by carefully balancing himself, he pulled off his shirt and threw it over the angry cat, neatly wrapping him up in the heavy fabric before carefully jumping down to the ground.

"Your cat." He handed her the wiggling bundle even though his expression told her he wouldn't have minded dropping it.

Letitia unwrapped the shirt and examined the cat, who continued to vent his frustration by telling her everything that happened to him in his ear-splitting yowls.

"Le Chat, we both have a lot to learn," she told the cat as she handed Tyler's shirt back to him. She tried hard not to stare at his impressive bare chest. "Thank you very much for getting him down."

"You're welcome." He didn't sound the least bit gracious. He examined the shirt that now sported new tears in the heavy fabric. "Although I don't think your cat is very grateful."

"I'll replace the shirt," she offered.

His gaze sliced right through her. "You're broke, countess, remember?"

Her face flamed. "I'm not destitute," she whispered. "And I would appreciate it if you wouldn't say that in front of people. It won't help matters any if they think their boss can't pay their salaries."

Tyler leaned down until his face was close to hers. "Well, I wouldn't worry too much since they'll probably find out soon enough when you can't sign their paychecks, won't they?"

Letitia opened her mouth to say something then snapped it shut. Still carrying her cat, she turned on her heel and stalked back to the house.

"That's her?" One of the men gave a low appreciative whistle. "Man, I hear those Italian dames are hot stuff. She sure looks it, doesn't she?"

Tyler's killing glare caught the man. "Let's get something clear, here and now. Anyone who opens their dirty mouth about Mrs. DeMarco will find themselves outta here and they might not be walking at the time, either. She's our boss, and we will give her the respect she's due. Understood?"

"Not if one of us wins the pool," one of the other men called out.

"What did you put in?" Tyler asked, fearing this was getting out of control and hating Letitia for even starting this. That crazy Giancarlo was bad enough, but he didn't have the build Letitia did, nor smell as good. He wiped from his mind the traitorous memory of her body falling against his in the truck.

"Thirty-two hours, ten minutes."

"Then you're still in the running." He shrugged his shirt back on and headed for the house. He didn't see any sign of Letitia in the main rooms but could hear her heels clicking on the bare wood floors and the musical sound of her voice as she talked to her cat. He kept a wary eye out for the cat as he walked down the hallway leading to the bedrooms.

"Some of this furniture is ruined from neglect. Hopefully, I can save some of the other pieces," he heard her murmur to Le Chat. He could visualize the killer cat nestled in her arms as she explored each bedroom. He grinned as he imagined her reaction when she reached the master bedroom at the end of the hall. She didn't disappoint him. "Oh my God!"

"Yep, right on the money." He chuckled, quickening his pace down the hallway. "What's wrong?" He kept his voice and expression carefully innocent.

Letitia's eyes were huge as she spun around. "That is disgusting!" She inclined her head toward the large four-poster bed, especially the wall over the head of the bed.

Tyler stared at the painting that graced the room. "I'll be damned," he breathed then burst out laughing.

"I'm glad you think it's funny." Letitia allowed Le Chat to jump down from her arms.

Considering she'd been married to an Italian, he was surprised she was such a prude. No wonder she wore white! "I'm sorry if you're offended by Harvey's idea of art, but he obviously thought a great deal of it since he hung it over his bed."

"Offended? I'm offended he had such atrocious taste." She gestured toward the dust-covered painting of a reclining nude woman draped in transparent veils. "That kind of artwork belongs more in a saloon than in a man's bedroom. Although, as you said, it must have had personal meaning to him. At least, I hope it did."

"Personal enough since the lady was his wife."

"His wife?" Letitia walked over for a closer look. "He allowed his wife to be painted nude?"

"I guess so, although the only pictures I ever saw of Harvey's wife she was fully clothed and about eighty pounds heavier," Tyler replied, shifting his gaze to Letitia. "How do you do it?"

The shift in conversation unbalanced her. "Do what?"

"This entire house is covered with dust and you're still spotless in that white outfit." He looked at her from head to foot.

She looked down. "Lucky, I guess. To be honest, I just don't attract dirt. When my brother moved into his horror of a mansion, the place was populated with the worst spiderwebs and creepy crawly things I'd ever seen but I was able to walk through unscathed. The workmen refused to even enter some of the rooms because they thought they were haunted by Humphrey Williams, the original owner of the house. Humphrey had a horrible reputation of scaring people off."

"It sounds like he didn't scare you off."

She shrugged, the gesture as graceful as everything else she did. "He tried but didn't succeed."

Tyler couldn't help but be fascinated by her story. "How did he try?"

Letitia's rose-glossed lips curved in a smile. "Humphrey was a bit of a voyeur. Jack said it was my imagination, but I just know the old boy watched me undress every evening. I guess even dead men have to get their kicks." She took one more look at the painting and wrinkled her nose. "That's one of the first things to go. I think I'd rather look at a picture of dogs playing pool than this."

His brows knitted together in a frown. "You're going to stay here?"

She looked around. "Despite all the dirt, this room is in the best shape. Or will be as soon as I clean it up."

He burst out laughing. "*You*, clean?"

"I am a very versatile woman, Mr. Barnes," Letitia informed him. "I can do whatever I put my mind to."

He chuckled. "Yeah, we'll see." He walked out of the room. "Although I admit I can't wait to see you looking grimy, countess," he tossed over his shoulder.

"Don't hold your breath, Barnes." She began to sit down on the bed then caught herself just in time. "That man will be the death of me yet."

"That woman is making me crazy," Tyler muttered, stalking out of the house and bellowing orders that the rest of Letitia's luggage be stored inside the house. It only took one look at their boss's dark features to prompt the men to obey him without question.

LETITIA'S NEXT DISCOVERY was that the water faucets yielded a rusty-looking sludge that didn't resemble anything even close to water. Before she could decide whether to just give in and scream her lungs out or sit down for a good cry, rattling sounds from the rear of the house caught her curiosity. She followed the sounds to the rear of the house where she found an immaculate-looking kitchen and a tall woman standing in front of the sink peeling carrots, her faded housedress was covered by a white apron. She sang along with the radio in a voice that could offend anyone's ears.

"Excuse me." Letitia ventured, still feeling shell-shocked as she looked around a large ultra clean kitchen and down at a floor that looked clean enough to eat off of, then gazed at gleaming counters. "Who are you?"

The woman turned around. "You must be the new owner." She had a no-nonsense manner. "I'm Myrna, the cook and I'm just that. I don't clean, I don't do laundry." She looked over Letitia's silk outfit. "I don't do fancy mending, just cooking and keeping this sorry excuse for a kitchen in working order."

Letitia nodded. Myrna might not look like her brother's housekeeper, Mrs. Boggs, but she had the New England woman's terse manner down pat.

"Meals are served at five, twelve-thirty and six," Myrna continued. "Anyone's late, they wait till the next meal. I'm not running no hotel here, there's no room service, and if anyone wants to eat any other time, they have to cook it and they have to clean up. But I'd prefer they do neither."

Letitia stifled her groan. She never thought of herself as a morning person. "I gather that five is five a.m.?"

"Of course it is!" the woman barked. "You may own this place, but the kitchen is my territory." She glared at Letitia to back up her words. "Got it?"

"Loud and clear," Letitia said in a tiny voice. "I, ah, was trying to run a bath, but the water..." She grimaced, holding up her hands to show defeat as she sneaked a look at the kitchen sink where clear water was running.

Myrna nodded her understanding. "I had the men dig a new well for the kitchen two years ago. That old one wasn't worth spit. Just have Tyler get some men on it." She turned back to peeling carrots.

Letitia's stomach rumbled but she wasn't about to ask if she could have a snack, even if she was willing to fix it for herself. Something told her the cook wouldn't appreciate anyone daring to invade her domain.

"I need to clean the master bedroom," she went on.

Myrna shook her head. "Girl, you'll ruin that fancy outfit of yours, but that's *your* problem. There's some cleaning supplies in that cupboard over there. Just put them back when you're finished." She turned her head and squinted at Letitia with faded blue eyes. "You really know how to clean?"

"How difficult can it be? I've seen the maids do it countless times," she countered, sounding more confident than she felt. She opened the cabinet Myrna indicated and found rags, furniture polish, glass cleaner and everything else she would need to restore the house to its former shining luster. She hoped.

Myrna shook her head again. "Lord help us from ignorant girls who probably don't know a dust mop from a dust rag."

Stung by the older woman's flat declaration, Letitia gathered up the supplies she would need. Carefully balancing rags, spray bottles and jars in her arms, she left the kitchen.

"If Mrs. Boggs could keep that enormous house clean, I should have no problem with one room," she murmured, making her way to the other end of the house with a disgruntled Le Chat trotting along at her heels.

"SO WHADDYA SAYING HERE, Tyler? That the lady spent all her cash buying this place sight unseen? Now come on, no woman is that crazy and believe me, in my sixty-two years on this earth, I've met all kinds." The grizzled man cornered Tyler in the barn the moment he'd entered.

"She's not crazy, J.T., just…" He racked his brain for the right description. Beautiful? Smells good? Looks like a million dollars? "Well, she kinda defies description."

The elderly man looked skeptical and knowing at the same time. "Yeah, I heard what she looks like. Young Ben's already acting like a puppy dog. And if you ain't careful, some of the hands are gonna be sniffin' around her like dogs sniffin' after a bitch in heat."

Tyler winced at the too apt description. "She's not what we expected," he blurted out.

J.T., ranch foreman until his sixtieth year when a fall from a horse broke his hip and hampered his activities, was the one to suggest Tyler take over his job. Now, he enjoyed spending days in the barn repairing tack, sitting on the porch and just being useful where needed. "Is she really some kind of Italian royalty?"

Tyler shook his head. "She's as American as you and me." He paused. "Well, actually, she's not," he amended. "She grew up in Europe, her brother's a renowned horror writer and she has a fancy cat that wears silk collars." He shook his head. "She's hard-headed, wears designer clothes unsuitable for ranch life and yet she seems to be determined to make a go of it out here."

"Then she doesn't know that Giancarlo promised to let you buy into the ranch?" J.T. asked as they walked away from the barn. He reached into his back pocket and pulled out a pack of cigarettes.

"It doesn't look like it." Tyler snatched the pack out of his hands. "You know very well the doctor told you to lay off those coffin nails. He said they were killing you, remember?"

J.T.'s profane reply told Tyler the older man's opinion of doctors. "They don't know spit," he growled, snatching the pack back. "'Sides, you're only complaining cause you gave 'em up last year but you're still yearnin' for one." ·

"Not a bit," he lied without a qualm.

J.T. changed the subject. "Let's get back to what we were talkin' about and off my smoking habits." A thought occurred to him. "Did she meet Myrna?"

Tyler shuddered. Few people intimidated him. The plainspoken cook was one of them. "If so, the countess will be off the property by nightfall and be more than willing to sell it to me."

J.T. took his time lighting his cigarette. "How long you bet she'd stay here?"

His mouth twitched. "She should have given up about an hour ago, but the lady is stubborn. I have a horrible feeling she isn't going to beg to be taken back to the airport so she can return to her big city and bright lights."

J.T.'s eyes were too knowing as he gazed at his one time protégé. "You be careful, boy," he advised, waving his cigarette at Tyler. "It sounds like that gal could tie you up in knots if you don't watch yourself."

Tyler looked off into the distance. He didn't want to admit to even J.T. that he feared Letitia DeMarco with the honey colored hair and flashing aqua eyes already had him tied up in knots.

"Considering the way things are going already, I'd say you could call it more a cross between heaven and hell, J.T.," he murmured. "My money's on it turning into more hell than heaven before this is over."

Chapter Three

Letitia viewed the dark musty cavern called the master-bedroom closet with the same trepidation she felt when she viewed a haunted Salem house more than a year ago.

"If I could whip a haunted house into shape, a dark and dank closet should be a piece of cake," she told herself as she backed away from the closet. She began to sit on the bed and checked herself just in time. The comforter, which might have had a lovely print at one time, was now a dingy gray.

"There is no way I can put clothing in there until it is much cleaner," she concluded, looking back inside with great caution. She looked at the pile of cleaning supplies at her feet. She doubted all of them together were strong enough to handle such a daunting task. "Which one should I begin with? And which one will banish all that nasty dirt?" She picked up one pump-action bottle of a pine-scented cleaner. "I seem to recall commercials saying you were very handy in getting rid of dirt. Let's find out if they were right."

After Letitia had left the kitchen, she'd returned to the master bedroom to change into more suitable clothing before cleaning the room. Since old clothing wasn't something she owned, the best she could come up with was a pair of melon-colored shorts with a melon and pale green print blouse that skimmed her waist.

"You looking for something in particular or just waiting for the maid to come in and put everything away before running your bath?"

She turned so suddenly her hair whipped in front of her face. She pushed the strands away from her eyes and reached for a band to pull it up into a loose ponytail.

"Do you enjoy frightening people out of their wits? As for a bath, after viewing the sludge you call water, I think I'll pass." She raised her arms to pull her hair through the band.

Tyler braced his shoulder against the doorjamb looking as if he had all the time in the world to waste. Except his eyes were riveted on the enticing sight of bare flesh revealed between the rising hem of her blouse and shorts. "Those are pretty fancy duds to clean in, countess," he noted, casting a lazy gaze over the rest of her form and clearly liking what he saw. "Those little shorts silk?"

She lifted her chin that necessary inch. "I normally don't clean, I delegate, but I'm sure I can handle it. After all, many women do it every day of their lives and I haven't heard of any casualties."

"Yeah, well, something tells me you're not just any woman." He kept his eyes focused on her bare legs.

You better believe it, buster! Letitia's lips curved in an amused smile. If he hoped to disconcert her by visually stripping her, he was going to learn better men than him had tried over the years and failed miserably!

"Shouldn't you be out overseeing the men punching cows and branding them or whatever you do out there?" she asked. "After all, isn't that what a foreman does?"

Tyler's lips compressed in a tight line to keep the laughter from spilling out. "Yeah, we do have a nasty habit of beating up those little doggies off and on," he drawled. "When we're not castrating them, that is."

Letitia's eyes widened at the idea. She suddenly felt a bit queasy. "All right, so I don't know a lot about ranch life, but I'm a quick study." She bent down to pick up a bottle of lemon oil and a dust rag, not even noticing she still held the bottle of pine cleaner.

"Going to polish the closet?"

"I'm just using whatever will get rid of those cobwebs." She repressed a shudder as she set the lemon oil down and spritzed cleaner on the cloth. Then she changed her mind and walked into the closet, spraying it everywhere she could reach. "It appears any house I'm in has these nasty things. There's probably a ghost lurking somewhere in here too." Her voice was muffled as she ventured farther inside the closet. She was grateful the light inside still worked.

"If it's Harvey, I wouldn't worry. He's a pretty easygoing guy." Tyler tipped his head to one side to catch a better view of her shapely buttocks as they swayed to some private rhythm. "This is just a suggestion, mind you, but why don't you use the dust mop? The long handle would mean you wouldn't have to get inside there and breathe in all those years of dust and you could still get a majority of the dirt out."

Letitia's loud coughs proceeded her escape from the dirty cavern. "A dust mop? With a long handle?" She glared at him as if this was all his fault.

"I'm sure Myrna has one."

Letitia's mutters closely resembled curses on Tyler's entire family as she pushed him to one side.

"Was it something I said?" Faint amusement colored his amiable question.

She spun to a stop and glowered at him.

"I can handle ranch foremen who look upon me as some flighty socialite who's out here on a whim. I can also handle cooks who boast a job description that doesn't take them beyond the kitchen door. What I cannot handle are people who look down on others just because they might not be familiar with something they've grown up around. I may not understand the western life-style, but that doesn't mean I can't learn it." Her eyes, the color of aqua gemstones, snapped with lively anger. "And I will learn it, Mr. Ranch Foreman. You can count on it."

He tipped his hat in reply to her challenge. "I'm looking forward to it, ma'am."

Letitia started toward the stairs then looked over her shoulder. "Was there something else you needed?"

He thought of the healthy whiff of perfume he got when she brushed past him. Amazing how the potent pine cleaner didn't have a chance against French perfume. His body tightened in sexual reaction. The lady had endured a long plane ride, an even longer truck ride on a not so smooth road and now she was preparing to clean house! Where did she get all this energy? He figured it had to be from all the fancy parties she attended over the years. Dancing and drinking French champagne all night could be wearing on the body if you weren't in good shape. "Not just yet, countess, but I'll be sure and let you know when I do."

Letitia's fingers lingered on the wall as she paused. She shot him a look over her shoulder that positively sizzled. Her eyes danced with wicked lights and her lips curved in the kind of smile that left Tyler aching to cover with his own mouth.

"Don't take too long, cowboy." To his ears, her husky voice made some pretty interesting unspoken promises. With a saucy twitch of her butt, she sauntered off.

Tyler took off his hat and wiped his forehead with the back of his hand. He wasn't surprised to find it had come away damp. "Damn," he muttered, replacing his hat with the intention of getting out of there as soon as possible. "Why couldn't she have climbed back in that plane and gotten out of here before I smelled that perfume!"

"YOU HAVE TO STOP laughing, Jack!" Letitia ordered her brother as she fingered piles of dust-covered papers on a desk she was certain came over by covered wagon more than a hundred years ago, in a room that she supposed to be the office only because of the journals piled in a sagging bookcase and a battered metal filing cabinet in one corner. "It's not that funny."

"You spent the afternoon cleaning your bedroom. Ticia, before today, your idea of housecleaning was making your bed and picking up your damp towels in the bathroom. And now, you're cleaning and talking about running a ranch. What do you even know about ranching?"

She gritted her teeth. "I can ride a horse."

"You can, *what?*" he teased.

"I *can* ride a horse and you know it! I just don't like them. I know cattle turn into steaks, I can read books on the subject and I'm a very quick learner. Besides, I have a very qualified foreman who can teach me what I don't know. Giancarlo even said he was one of the best in the state although I can't understand why the ranch is doing so badly if he's supposed to be so good."

Giancarlo just never said that the man had a chest a woman itched to caress, eyes that should be considered illegal and looked like something out of the old wild west.

"Giancarlo also took you for well over a hundred thousand dollars," Jack reminded her. "I can't imagine his word would exactly carry a lot of weight."

"The ranch is worth much more than that." Letitia thought about Tyler's unwelcome news that the ranch was virtually broke. Just as she was. She wondered how she managed to get into these situations. If she believed in such a thing, she'd think it had something to do with her karma.

"Ticia, do you need anything?" Jack asked during her long silence.

She knew he meant money. "No, everything is fine," she brightly replied, perhaps too brightly. "Although I could use some reference materials to help me understand this part of the country."

"What do you need?"

Letitia rattled off a list that sent her brother into waves of laughter. "It's not that funny!" she argued.

"It will be if your employees find out how you're learning about the West and ranch life," he said, chuckling. "All right, I'll send you whatever I can find by the end of the week. But Ticia—" he took a deep

breath "—don't feel bad if you have to leave there.
You can always come back here, you know. Holly and
the kids would love to have you back."

The pull was strong to confess to her brother that
ranch life was already turning into a passel of unpleasant surprises. She even opened her mouth to say
just that, but something held her back.

"Everything is fine, Jack," she assured him. "And
I would appreciate anything you can send me. My love
to Holly, Caroline and Ryan." She hung up before she
gave into the need to beg her brother to come take her
back to Salem. She couldn't call it home; it was her
brother's home. Actually, if Letitia thought about it,
this was the first time she had a place she could call all
hers. Even when she was married she didn't live in her
own home. She and Stephano had shared a suite in the
family mansion. He saw no need to buy a house when
the suite was larger than many people's homes.

"All mine," she murmured, looking around at
more piles of newspapers, old receipts, bills she hoped
had been paid and a journal she discovered was a day-
to-day account of the work done. It was the owner's
office. And now her office. The thought was downright scary. She collapsed in the leather chair, dis-
turbing another pile of dust. She sneezed several times
and waved the flying molecules away from her face.
"If I tap my heels together three times and ask to go
home, will it happen?"

On a whim, she did just that. Letitia opened one
eye, then the other. She sighed. "I guess I *am* home."

She jumped up when she heard voices coming from
the rear of the house. A quick glance at her watch told
her she was in danger of missing dinner and her rum-

bling stomach warned her that wouldn't be a good idea.

Letitia brushed her clothing with her hands and swiped at stray hairs as she hurried down the hall to the kitchen. Her bright smile wavered when she encountered a long table in the adjoining dining room filled with men who looked at her with varied forms of curiosity. The braver ones ventured more than a few looks at her bare legs. She wished she'd now taken the time to change into pants. Or checked a mirror to see if there was dirt on her nose.

"Good evening," she greeted them, calling on her finishing school training as she deliberately broadened her smile. She'd encountered heads of state, diplomats and royalty during her marriage and her few years of wandering the continent. If they couldn't rattle her composure, a bunch of cowhands shouldn't be able to. "I'm Letitia DeMarco."

"Ma'am." A gray-haired man nodded as he pushed his chair back and stood up. He shot a telling look up and down the table until all the chairs were pushed back and the men stood dipping their heads in silent greetings. "I'm J. T. Walker, the old man around here who refuses to retire. I look after the barns, handle the tack and watch over our pregnant mares."

A covert glance told Letitia that Tyler wasn't there.

"You gonna just stand there looking like a picture out of *Vogue* or are you gonna sit down and eat?" Myrna demanded, walking up behind her. She gestured toward the head of the table. "Guess that'll be your seat, as you're the boss."

"Thank you, Myrna." She walked to the head of the table and seated herself.

"Well, you've already met Ben," J.T. began, pointing to faces as he reeled off the names. "That's Sam, Chad, Tony," he went on, pausing each time to allow Letitia time to fit the name to the face. "Jake's over there."

She smiled and nodded at each man even if several of them didn't smile back at her with the same friendliness she accorded them.

"I'm sure it will take time for me to get to know all of you," she told them. "I realize I'm not Giancarlo."

"Wouldn't matter if you were. He never bothered coming out here to even look over the place," one of the men muttered into his coffee. "We were left to do what we know best without any interfering from folk who ride around in fancy cars and don't worry about anything more than what to wear to the next party. Don't know why he even bothered keeping the place."

Letitia's smile froze. "I'm not Giancarlo."

His eyes swept over her knit sleeveless top with cold insolence, stopping level with her breasts. "Yeah, I noticed."

"Chad," J.T. growled. "The lady is our boss."

Chad stood up. "I never signed on to work for a woman," he argued. "And I don't intend to work for some society dame."

Before Letitia could protest his words, another voice cut in with chilling precision. "Who said you were? Last I heard, you took my orders. That hasn't changed yet."

Tyler stopped long enough to hang his hat on the rack before walking over to take his seat. He kept his gaze centered on the other man. "You have any other complaints we should discuss?"

Chad's face tightened. He grabbed his chair and sat back down. "I'll let you know."

Tyler looked relaxed, as if he wasn't discussing anything more major than the weather. "You do that. We'll have a nice talk."

Letitia stared down at the coffee cup filled with the dark brew Myrna had poured. From the way the men were talking she began to wonder if a showdown at noon would be next. She mentally thanked the fates for modern cowhands not wearing guns to the table. She feared she wouldn't be able to dive under the table fast enough.

"Eat up." Myrna set platters filled with sizzling steaks, fried potatoes and vegetables at each end of the table. A large covered basket filled with biscuits was next.

"If you're slow, you'll lose out," Tyler advised her, forking up one of the smaller steaks and dropping it on her plate.

"I usually eat a light dinner," she demurred.

"For us, this is light," he explained. "Our main meal is at dinnertime. You call it lunch in the city."

She nodded, reaching for the potatoes just as the bowl was swept away.

Letitia decided it would be best to remain quiet and just listen as the men slowly relaxed and began talking about the day's work and what was planned for the next day. She mentally filed away phrases about post holes, fencing, vaccinations. Considering how many times the men would cough or pause while talking, she assumed they were also censuring their language in deference to her presence. She'd never felt so much like a fifth, and very unwanted, wheel. Even Tyler gave her little more than a few cursory glances as he ate. She might as well not have been there.

Except Letitia noticed Tyler more than she would have liked to. He'd changed into a clean shirt since she last saw him and after seeing a few damp ringlets of hair against his nape, she figured he'd also showered and shaved. A normal occurrence before dinner? Or in her honor? She felt even grubbier and wished she'd done more than just wash her hands.

After making room where there wasn't any for berry cobbler, Letitia wanted nothing more than to curl up in a corner and go to sleep. She was jolted out of her stupor when Tyler stood up.

"Is there a chance we could talk?" she asked, mentally slapping her cheeks to wake herself up.

He stared down at her for a moment. Just when she thought he was going to put her off, he replied. "All right." He gestured for her to precede him.

Letitia mentally ran down her choices and found all of them wanting. "The office?"

"You're the boss."

His sardonic tone followed her down the hallway.

"To begin with, I wonder if I might have a daily report on what you have the men do," she began, once seated behind the desk. "I thought it might be a good way to familiarize myself with the ranch and what goes on here."

Tyler was grateful the bulky desk kept Letitia's legs out of sight. They were long and smooth and a pale gold color and they kept his mind wandering in their direction when he should be concentrating on how to talk her into selling him the ranch!

"The best way for you to do that is to ride with the men and observe things firsthand," he advised.

Letitia's face froze. "Ride?"

Tyler perched himself on the chair arm. "Yeah, ride. Of course, we don't have any fancy English saddles, countess, but I'm sure we can fix you up. You can ride, can't you?"

She was stung by his mocking challenge. "Of course I can ride! It's just not one of my favorite activities," she added quietly unwilling to divulge one of her pet peeves. Her ex-husband, most of her friends and even her brother enjoyed horseback riding. She always considered it a way of getting seasick without being on board a ship.

Tyler shook his head in disbelief. "You now own a working ranch and you don't like to ride? There's a lot of territory that can't be reached by jeep, countess. How did you expect to look over your land? By private airplane?"

"I said I didn't like horses, not that I couldn't ride them!" she argued, then took several deep breaths to regain her rapidly diminishing composure. "Look, I know I'm not what you expected."

"No joke there," he said under his breath.

Letitia glared at him. "But you could go a little easier on me. This is all new to me. Before today, my idea of a cattle ranch was what I saw on reruns of 'Bonanza.' I freely admit I'm a novice at this. All I'm asking is for you to give me a chance to learn. Now, the first thing I'd like to learn is why this ranch isn't doing very well. In most companies, that kind of problem is usually related to management."

Letitia firmly believed in body language telling her a great deal. Tyler was still perched on the arm of a chair as if not wanting to take the time to take a proper seat. His arms crossed in front of his chest told her loud and clear that he wasn't pleased with her.

"What exactly did Giancarlo tell you about this place?" he asked quietly, fury etched in his features.

She mulled over his question before replying. "Just the usual social chitchat one night how he'd bought the ranch about five years ago as a tax shelter."

"Meaning he needed a tax loss and we were the perfect setup."

She winced at his blunt observation. "I'm sure he wanted people to think that. The problem is, Giancarlo didn't have enough money to his name to require a tax shelter." Her lips tightened fractionally then relaxed as if she knew what her expression was giving away. "All he has to his name *is* his name, an impressive family tree, who have disowned him by the way, a great deal of charm, good looks and the ability to live off other people," she spoke candidly. "He's the worst kind of con artist because he'll never get caught."

Tyler wasn't surprised to hear that piece of news. "He never bothered with the place. I'd write or call and tell him what needed to be done. He'd say he'd get back to me, but he never did. I'm not making excuses. I'm just stating the facts." Facts he didn't like bringing up.

"Giancarlo could lie with the best of them," she explained. "That's why he's done so well in his endeavors."

"Every crook gets caught sooner or later," Tyler pointed out. "It just takes longer for some to take a fall than others."

"It doesn't happen if the victims refuse to prosecute," Letitia softly countered. "The rich hate to be bilked, even in a small way. And the rich who've had money for more years than the earth has been around hate to have it be known someone got past all their built-in defenses. Instead, they invite Giancarlo in for a private meeting and offer him a reasonable settlement to keep quiet about it and most of the time, to even leave town. He's been steadily working his way west using that method. He can't return to Italy because his family doesn't want him, either. They pay him a tidy sum to stay away and he doesn't want to lose that steady income by defying their orders."

"And what did he get out of you?"

She should have known he'd figure it out. "He thought marrying me would give him a nice piece of Stephano's alimony since it would have continued even if I remarried. It was part of my settlement. Unfortunately for him, one of his less friendly victims happened to show up at a party and after a few glasses of champagne she told anyone who would listen what he was like. I was one of those who listened and believed what she said." She shrugged as if it was of little consequence. She wasn't going to tell him she'd literally held Giancarlo at gunpoint to obtain ownership of the ranch since he couldn't repay the money he'd stolen from her.

"Is your poor-little-me tale supposed to make me feel sorry enough for you that I'll cut you some slack?"

Letitia's eyes blazed a fire that should have turned Tyler into a crispy critter.

"When you hire a new man, don't you give him a chance to show you what he can do?" she demanded.

"When I hire a man the first thing I know is what he can do. If he wants a job here, he'll have the references and the know-how." He fixed her with a telling stare that said loud and clear she didn't have either. "We don't have the time around here to train anyone green. This is a working ranch, not a prep school. If they don't have the know-how, they can look elsewhere."

Stung by his words, Letitia jumped to her feet and stalked around the desk until she stood in front of him. Her fingers tightened into tiny fists then straightened out. Tyler watched her with a cautious eye. He knew those dangerous-looking nails could prove lethal if she so chose. Painted nails that didn't have one chip in the polish or one broken tip. How does she do it? The woman did heavy-duty chores for a couple of hours, yet her hands looked as if they hadn't done more than serve afternoon tea.

"Then I gather you feel the need to set those same standards for a new owner." Sarcasm laced her voice as she stared him down. "Why not hold interviews, check references, maybe hand out a few skill tests? How did Giancarlo do on your little interview?" she challenged, deliberately stepping into his space. His narrowed eyes told her just how much he disliked her doing that. Her blazing ones told him she was glad. And that she could push even more.

Tyler's jaw tightened. "Lady, you're pushing it."

"Mister, you ain't seen nothing yet."

Her lazy drawl was just enough to push him over that razor's edge. Tyler stood up hoping the movement would force Letitia to step back. He should have known better. She hadn't backed down yet. Why should she start now?

"So when do you want to start the interview?" she dared, sticking her chin out.

"Right now."

He was past thinking straight, thanks to her. Instead, he'd just show her. With his hands gripping her shoulders, he pulled her against him and lowered his head. The moment his mouth covered hers, he knew he was in trouble. The lady tasted like the sweetest of sins and headiest of delights. And she kissed him back with the kind of enthusiasm that made his jeans feel about six sizes too small.

"Damn you, countess." He ground out the words against her slightly parted lips. The fact that her aqua eyes were already cloudy with desire didn't escape him. "The first minute I saw you I should have known you were trouble." Her fragrance surrounded him in a perfumed cage. "So go ahead, take your shot at knocking my head off. That's what you're looking to do, isn't it?"

Letitia looked at him for a long moment. Tyler braced himself for the first blow. He knew there was no way she wasn't going to get even with him for that kiss. And he wanted to be prepared for the worst.

Her arms flowed languidly up around his neck. She wrapped her soft hands around his nape and just as slowly pulled his face back down to hers.

"Fasten your seat belt, cowboy," she murmured, latching on to his lower lip with her teeth and gently pulling it between her lips. "You're in for the kind of ride no wild bronco could give you."

Chapter Four

Steam was pouring out of his ears. Tyler just knew clouds were snaking their way up to the ceiling. Every nerve in his body felt ready to explode at any moment. And why shouldn't they be going off like rockets? He had a beautiful woman in his arms who knew just how to push all the right buttons. And she did it very well, too.

Letitia alternately nibbled on his lower lip and grazed her teeth across the tender underside. Her sensual feasting was interspersed with throaty murmurs that sent his blood pressure skyrocketing, along with certain parts of his body.

"I want you to think about this, cowboy. Right now, you have more woman in your arms than you'll ever have," she breathed, combing her fingers through the hair lying against his shirt collar. "I'm talking one hundred percent, grade A female. So you better enjoy what you've got because you probably won't get this lucky ever again." She dotted his chin with tiny kisses as she whispered, "Got that?"

"Countess, believe me, I know not only what to do when I'm holding prime merchandise, but I'll make sure you enjoy it as much as I do." He widened his stance so that she was held fast against the cradle of his hips. He angled his head so he could better taste the shell-like spiral of her ear.

Letitia murmured a sigh of delight as Tyler's tongue curved around her ear. "Oh, yes," she breathed, "you most definitely know how to enjoy."

"Not only that, countess." His teeth bore down on her earlobe and nibbled around the blue topaz stud earrings she wore. "But I know a con job when I see one. I may be a country boy, but I can tell when a big city woman is trying out her seduction skills on me. You're good, very good, but just remember this. In this kind of game there can only be one winner. That means someone has to lose. I *never* lose." He released her by dropping his arms and stepping back. Before a stunned Letitia could think of anything to say he'd tipped his hat to her and walked out of the room.

She collapsed against the edge of the desk. "Well, that was certainly informative," she murmured, fanning her hot face with her hand. "If I'd known country boys were such good kissers, I would have exchanged Italy for the rural life long ago."

THE CLOCK MUST BE WRONG. It had to be wrong! Letitia rolled over and slapped at the annoying buzz coming from the nightstand. She opened one eye, groaned and dragged the pillow over her head.

"It's still dark outside. No one in their right mind gets up when it's dark outside. You can't see what you're doing."

They do if you want coffee and you know very well you're not worth spit until you've had your morning ration of caffeine.

A soft moan left her lips. "Terrific, now my mind is even talking like something out of a western."

Letitia forced herself out of bed. She would have preferred taking a shower, but after a look at the clock she knew she would have to hurry. She doubted Myrna had been kidding about the mealtimes.

As she pulled on a lightweight tunic sweater and brushed her hair up into a loose ponytail, she glanced out the window. Lights blazed from a two-story building that she took to be the bunkhouse. Men walked out of the open front door, most of them smothering yawns. Beyond that she could see the barn, also lit up inside. A tiny sound caught her attention.

"Poor Le Chat," she cooed, picking up her cat and holding him close to her. "This is all new to you too, isn't it? As much as I'd like to stay here and cuddle you until you feel secure, I need my coffee more, so let's get you dressed, too." She opened a small leather case and rummaged through the contents. A silk collar in the same blue as her sweater was quickly fastened around the cat's neck. "So, my love, how do you think the foreman will greet me today?" She kept her cat in her arms as she headed toward the source of the enticing aroma of coffee. She sighed. "Something tells me he won't be in the same mood he was last night."

The men fell into a charged silence when Letitia walked in with Le Chat hot on her heels. The cat stalked over to the stove and sat down looking expectantly at Myrna waiting to be served.

"Good morning," she greeted them with a cheery smile.

"I don't allow animals in my kitchen." Myrna eyed Le Chat suspiciously.

"Oh, Le Chat isn't an animal," Letitia assured her.

"Hell, no, Myrna, that cat's descended from royalty," Tyler drawled, walking inside. His smile for the cook was warm. It turned much cooler when it fell on Letitia. She refused to allow her own smile to waver. "We need to treat it real special."

The cat narrowed his eyes, the same color as Letitia's, and hissed at Tyler. The cat then turned his back in cold dismissal, raised his tail to curl over his back and walked off with the manner of one dusting his hands of a nasty problem.

"'Pears the lady's cat isn't too fond of you, boy." J.T. chuckled, shuffling inside.

"That cat isn't real," he muttered darkly, heading for the table. "Well, boss lady, any orders for the day?"

Letitia welcomed his challenge for what it was.

"I'm sure you all have figured out my knowledge of ranching could fit on the head of a pin with plenty of room to spare." She dared to invade Myrna's pantry hunting for a can of tuna. Once her cat was fed his breakfast, she sat in the chair she'd used the night before and poured herself a cup of coffee. "I'm hoping no one will mind if I just play the part of observer for a while."

"Even on horseback?" Tyler spoke up.

"Even on horseback," she answered his dare.

"You boys don't need to worry about the little lady," J.T. rumbled. "I'll take care of her."

If any of the other men were going to offer their services, their offers died the moment they saw the warning look on their boss's face. All ducked their heads and studiously applied themselves to their breakfast.

"The lady is my responsibility," Tyler broke in, not sounding the least enthusiastic about the idea.

J.T.'s eyes held mild amusement as he gazed at his boss. "That she is, but I know you had some major plans for this morning. How about I show her around the barns while you do that and you take over after?"

Tyler's mouth thinned. "You have your own work to worry about."

"Excuse me?" Letitia held up her hand and waved it to get his attention. "But don't I have any say in this?"

"No." Tyler didn't bother looking at her.

Her eyes turned a stormy blue-green at his curt reply. She opened her mouth, fully prepared to blast the man to smithereens. As if he sensed her coming retaliation, Tyler turned his head and settled a be-quiet-or-suffer-the-consequences gaze on her.

Letitia settled back in her seat, telling herself the only reason she wasn't saying anything was that she didn't want to cause a scene in front of the men. She settled for nibbling her toast, pretending she was tearing into Tyler's tough hide.

No man should look that good! Especially first thing in the morning when she'd barely had time to brush her teeth. Considering Myrna's pointed look at the wall clock when Letitia walked into the kitchen, she was glad she'd hurried through her shower instead of taking her time under the thin stream of lukewarm clear water that appeared five minutes after she turned it on. As it was, she would need to find a plumber to work on the antiquated plumbing.

"We've got a full day ahead of us," Tyler stated to no one in particular. He stood up and moved toward the door without a backward glance.

The men didn't waste any time in taking his less than subtle hint. Only J.T. remained behind. He lounged in his chair, nursing his cup of coffee as he traded jokes with Myrna while she cleared the table.

"Do you need any help?" Letitia ventured.

The older woman didn't look up as she loaded the dishwasher. "The kitchen is my domain. I've been doing this myself for the past twenty-three years. I intend to keep it that way."

J.T. smiled at Letitia and winked. "Better listen. That's one where her bite's as bad as her bark," he whispered.

Letitia's lips curved. "Then I'll just hope I've had all the necessary shots," she whispered back.

J.T. finished his coffee and stood up. "Why don't you come out to the barn in about a half hour?" he suggested as he slowly rose to his feet.

She grinned. "I'll be there."

He grinned back. "Just make sure you wear shoes that won't mind getting a mite dirty."

Bemused, Letitia watched him leave. "What a darling!"

Myrna rolled her eyes. "He's a crusty old man." She looked down at Le Chat who sat on his haunches watching her with unblinking eyes. "That cat's fur really that color or did ya have it dyed to match your hair?"

"It was easier to have mine changed." Letitia carried her mug over to the sink. "Besides, I had the shade of blond hair that could only be considered dishwater blond. I was very happy to change it."

Myrna held a dishcloth under the running water and wrung it out. "You really intend to make a go of it here?"

"I'd like the chance to try even if Tyler doesn't think I can," she replied. "I asked my brother to send some things out to me in hopes they'll help."

The older woman looked at her tunic sweater and leggings. "You might want to change into jeans before you head out to the barn. Something you don't mind getting dirty, at least—ruined, at most."

Letitia wrinkled her nose. "I don't have any jeans. For the time being, I'll have to stick to my more casual outfits like this one. I'm not that worried about anything getting ruined."

"You'd better get some jeans. Fancy clothes like that won't last long around here. All they'll do is get the hands watching you more than watching what they're supposed to be doing," Myrna said bluntly. "And Tyler don't hold with any slackers around here. There's too much work to be done and not enough hours in the day to do it."

Letitia looked down at her laced fingers. "Giancarlo really didn't do anything for the ranch, did he?" She knew she'd get a straight answer from her. She knew what she heard from Tyler and she kept reminding herself she wasn't trying to verify his answer. She just wanted to hear it from another party. "He didn't bother checking on it, seeing if any changes could be made, anything like that."

"He didn't care what went on out here. That's when Tyler figured we were pretty much on our own and he did all he could to make the ranch at least pay for its own expenses. The only good thing Giancarlo did was promise Tyler he'd sell it to him when Tyler saved up enough money for a down payment and could swing a loan."

Shock froze Letitia to her spot. "No wonder he resents seeing me here," she murmured to herself. "I'm the thief who stole his dream." She turned away, feeling a little sick to her stomach. She understood much more then. "I guess I better get changed."

Myrna's stern features relaxed. It wasn't a true smile, but Letitia figured it was probably the closest the woman ever came to one. "Don't worry about Tyler. He's a fair man. He knows it isn't your fault he lost out on the ranch."

She never felt less like smiling. "Knowing and believing are two different things."

Letitia returned to her room with Le Chat scrambling at her heels. She quickly exchanged her pale blue leather ballet flats for a sturdier pair of loafers. They were of soft Italian glove leather and would not be the same after this morning. She didn't let it bother her though. By now, she was grimly determined to prove to Tyler she was worthy of running the ranch.

"No, I don't think you should come out with me." She stooped down and gently pushed Le Chat away from the door before the cat could streak outside. "I don't have any idea where that dog might be and I don't want anything to happen to you. Or to him," she added.

Letitia took her time as she walked along a well trod path that led to the barn. She stopped several times, lifting her head to the early summer sun and sniffing the air. Her smile grew broader as she looked around the empty expanse that she assumed was the backyard, if ranches had such a thing. The smile disappeared as she sadly gazed at the plot of dirt that she easily imagined green with lush grass and bordered with colorful flowers. Would it be that difficult to put some life into it? she wondered, her mind already racing a mile a minute with possibilities.

She shaded her eyes with her hand as she took in the nearby rolling hills dotted with cattle grazing. A thrill of pride ran through her body as she surveyed the quiet scene.

"It's mine," she murmured with quiet awe. "This is all mine." She couldn't stop smiling as she slowly turned in a circle.

"Lord, missy, the way you dawdle, you'll be lucky if you even see the first barn," J.T. called out from the open barn doorway where he stood watching her.

She turned around and walked to him. "There's no grass, no flowers out here."

He looked confused. "There's more than enough grass for the cattle. Probably cause we're not running the numbers we used to."

Letitia shook her head. "No, I mean there's no grass, no flowers right here." She swept her hand in a half circle toward the yard area.

"No reason to have any."

"No reason? There's always a reason to have flowers and even a small patch of grass," she argued.

He looked puzzled. "Why?"

Letitia opened her mouth then shut it again. "Why?" She needed to be sure she heard his question correctly.

He nodded.

She pulled in a deep breath. "Because they cheer people up, they add beauty to the area and..." She couldn't believe she'd run out of reasons so quickly! "And they add color."

J.T. shook his head as he led her into the dim interior. "There's no one around here who's got the time to take proper care of flowers. Not when there's a ranch this size to run. Tell me somethin', since you lived in Italy, did you ever meet Gina Lollobrigida? Now that's one fine woman!''

Letitia shook her head. "No, I'm sorry I never did. Although, it was rumored that my ex-father-in-law had a fling with her many years ago. I *did* see Sophia Loren at a charity ball once.''

He smiled. "Yep, she's another looker. The women today just don't have what the women back then had.''

She leaned against a stall door. She decided she liked the grizzled old man with the wry twinkle in his eye. "What did they have then that was so special?''

"They were *real* women,'' he stated. "They didn't care about all this equality nonsense because they didn't need to. They were women who took care of themselves, but knew how to make a man feel like a man when it counted.''

"Were you ever married, J.T.?'' Letitia asked curiously.

He shook his head. "Hell, when I was young I was too busy seein' the country to want to get tied down. By the time I took the job here, I was too settled in my ways to bother with a woman.''

"There's always Myrna.'' Her sly question hit its mark.

"Myrna's as set in her ways as I am in mine,'' he informed her. "And no matchmakin', missy, or you'll find yourself in a sorry patch of trouble.''

"I figured it wouldn't hurt,'' she teased, straightening up and following him through the barn.

Letitia walked into the tack room and fingered bridles hanging from various hooks. Many of them had been mended with intricate delicacy that defied the naked eye. She studied a saddle that was waiting for a broken cinch strap to be repaired.

"Giancarlo told me the ranch was a real money-maker." She sighed. "I should have known better. He hadn't told the truth about anything else. Why should he have about this? Especially when I was holding a gun on him." Seeing his curiosity, she relayed the story of how she received the ranch.

J.T. hooted and slapped his knee. "Bet that showed him." His expression sobered. "A money-*taker* is more like it. Ranching isn't a cheap operation. When the snows are heavy, we have to truck feed out to the cattle which is damn expensive if you don't grow your own. While we can handle most of our own animal doctoring, there's some things we need a vet out here for, then there's the pay for the men, food, and that's not takin' into account doctor bills if one of the men gets hurt."

Letitia experienced a sinking feeling. "Give me an estimate." The figure J.T. quoted sent her stomach falling into a bottomless pit. "Is there anything positive you can tell me?"

J.T. pondered her question. "We ain't been fore-closed on yet."

"That's a heartening thought."

By the time J.T. finished showing Letitia through the barns where she admired two new colts, a new-born filly and listened to J.T.'s comments about the ranch, her head was whirling with information and going crazy over the facts and figures he tossed out.

"What have I gotten myself into?" she moaned, leaning against a corral fence.

"Mind telling me something?" J.T. asked.

She held her hand up, palm out. "Yes, I did take a vow that I will never allow myself to be lured by the charms of an Italian man again. And I should have shot him when I had the chance."

He grinned. "No, I just wondered if you're going to stick it out."

"I have no choice."

"Everyone has a choice."

"I'm not everyone."

He eyed her leggings that weren't as immaculate as before. Bits of hay snagged the fabric beyond repair and several smudges of dirt dotted her sweater. "That I can see. So why?"

From the beginning, Letitia sensed she had a friend in the elderly man and opted to answer him honestly rather than with a flippant remark. "So I can prove I can succeed on my own."

He nodded. "You know, they don't think you can make it."

"They, meaning Tyler." She shrugged. "Then I'll just have to prove him wrong, won't I?" She stepped to one side and froze. She looked down at her now filthy shoe, grimaced and spat out a word.

J.T. chuckled. "If that word means what I think it does, you're right."

LETITIA WALKED BAREFOOT into the kitchen, after dumping her ruined shoes into the trash can set just outside the kitchen door.

"They might have been saved with a good dose of bleach and heavy-duty detergent," Myrna commented, having watched Letitia's progress across the yard.

She wrinkled her nose. "I don't think so."

"Then you better think about getting yourself a good pair of boots before all of your shoes start turning that particular shade of brown."

"Correct me if I'm wrong, but from what I've already deduced, a major mall isn't within driving distance."

"No, but the town has a store that carries everything a body needs and we also have a good bootmaker. Tyler has to drive into town this afternoon. He can take you."

"I can what?" The object of Myrna's offer roared loud enough to make Letitia jump.

"Take Letty into town for a pair of boots. Her shoes might be fine for inside the house, but she needs something sturdier for around the barn and for riding." Myrna was unperturbed by Tyler's glare.

Tyler looked down at Letitia. "Yeah, I heard you didn't look before you stepped. Not exactly a good idea when you're around horses who aren't housebroken."

She just wished he wasn't so blasted tall! And incredible. Now she knew what Holly meant when she once told Letitia just looking at Jack not only took her breath away but all sense of rational thought. Because Letitia most definitely felt it with Tyler. "Yes, I discovered that. Tomorrow they all have to start wearing diapers."

Tyler stared at Letitia, unsure if she was kidding or not.

She rolled her eyes. "It's a joke, all right? Just a very bad joke."

"She needs the boots, Tyler," Myrna spoke up.

"We'll leave right after dinner." He spoke directly to Letitia. "For all our sakes, don't wear high heels.

I'd hate to have you break your neck while climbing out of the truck."

"I could have figured that out on my own," she sputtered at his retreating back. "That man is so irritating and chauvinistic and..." She ran out of insults. "Neanderthal!"

Yeah, what a shame he's so good-looking to boot.

Letitia peeked out the window. From behind the starched curtains, she could watch Tyler's lean-hipped body saunter across the yard to the largest black stallion she'd ever seen.

"Naturally, he'd ride a big horse," she muttered, unaware every word was heard by a grinning Myrna. She watched him swing himself into the saddle. "I bet he thinks of his big horse just like any man thinks of a fast car. Both of them nothing more than a phallic symbol to make them feel macho."

"Honey, from what I've heard about Tyler and the ladies, he doesn't need to worry about any of those symbols. He does just fine all on his own."

Letitia grimaced. "Jack has told me countless times that I need to think before I speak. I'm just glad that glorified cowboy out there didn't hear me. Who knows what horrible reply he would have come up with."

Myrna cracked a smile. "He would have had some fun with you, that's for sure."

Yes, and Letitia was only too familiar with Tyler's idea of fun "I think I'll see what I can do to clear up some of that mess in the office." Letitia reluctantly pulled herself away from the window.

Myrna nodded. "Just keep an eye on the clock. I run these meals on a schedule, remember?"

"I'm sure if I didn't remember, my stomach would."

In the next hour and a half, Letitia made two very important discoveries. None of the paperwork was dated any later than ten years ago and Harvey's idea of bookkeeping was to stuff all the receipts in a journal and toss them in an envelope when they were paid.

"Something else I'll have the pleasure of asking the foreman," she said with a sigh, pushing herself away from the desk.

She looked around, making a mental note to bring in some boxes and clean out the desk. Except what should she keep and what should she throw out?

"Maybe I'd be better off if I just burned it all," she lamented, sorting the various pieces of paper into three piles—one to definitely be thrown away, one to find out from Tyler if they're important or not, and the last held papers she knew had to be kept. At dinnertime she looked at the piles, pleased with the progress she'd made.

When Letitia walked into the kitchen she found only J.T. and a couple of the other men at the table.

"When they're working out on the range, it's easier to take their meal with them," J.T. answered Letitia's inquiring look.

"I thought maybe I'd scared everyone away." She stopped by the butcher-block worktable and picked up a tureen of beef stew.

"Only that critter you call a cat could do that," Tyler spoke up as he entered the kitchen. He neatly plucked the tureen out of her hands and set it on the table.

"Do you do that for Myrna?" she questioned.

"When it's beef stew I do. I don't want to see her drop it and lose us a good dinner." He looked down at her feet. "You don't intend to wear those to town, do you?"

She followed his disdainful gaze. "Why not? They're shoes."

Tyler muttered a comment about God saving them from women who don't know what real shoes are.

Letitia studied her light blue leather ballet flats, twisting them one way then the other. "I wonder what you'll complain about next," she murmured.

"Just give me some time and I'll have a list for you."

As they ate their meal, Tyler couldn't stop sneaking glances at Letitia. He had to admit she didn't pick at her food the way so many women tended to nowadays. Considering the way she'd been eating since arriving at the ranch, he figured she had the kind of metabolism some women would kill for.

Letitia looked up just as she was about to spoon stew into her mouth. She gave a tiny embarrassed smile and put the spoon down. "I usually don't eat like this," she admitted. "It must be all the fresh air."

"I gave her a tour of all the barns this morning," J.T. told Tyler. "She's a quick learner."

Tyler's eyes dropped to Letitia's mouth. "Oh, I'm sure the lady has a lot of hidden talents she'll choose to reveal to us soon enough."

She refused to show any reaction to his pointed look and silent comment on the kind of woman he thought she was. No wonder! She had kissed his socks off, and given a little more encouragement, could have kissed a great deal more off than that! She noticed everyone was concentrating on their food and not even looking their way. She made sure the others couldn't see her as she turned to Tyler with a bold smile pasted on her lips. She waited until he sensed her eyes on him and looked up with an inquiring expression. The minute he did she pursed her lips and blew him a silent kiss. He didn't say a word. He didn't have to. The stunned look on his face gave her the answer she wanted.

Chapter Five

Letitia had accomplished a great deal more than she thought. Thanks to her erotic gestures, Tyler's hunger was rapidly being replaced by another hunger that couldn't be appeased by stew and dumplings.

He realized that in Letitia DeMarco, he'd found the one woman who seemed to know exactly what to do to unbalance him. Right now he wasn't sure whether to kiss her or throttle her. The latter was winning the battle raging inside his head while his nervous system was fighting for the former. He stood up with an abrupt jerk of his body and pushed back his chair.

"We'll leave in ten minutes." He didn't look at Letitia as he spoke. "If you're not ready, I leave without you." He walked out without a backward glance.

"I'm surprised Mr. Personality didn't want us to synchronize our watches," Letitia huffed. J.T.'s rusty chuckle caught her attention. She glared at him. "Did you say something?"

He shook his head, his lips still twitching. "No ma'am. I figure more than enough has been said already and I like my head right where it is."

Letitia turned to Myrna whose own shoulders were shaking with silent laughter at the exchange. "Cowboys are crazy."

"Yes, I guess they are," Myrna agreed. "Except you couldn't find a better breed of man when you need one."

Letitia didn't quite agree. She deliberately dawdled over her meal, but she still kept a close eye on the clock. She wouldn't give him any excuse to leave her behind. She knew he'd be out the door in a flash if she gave him the opportunity.

"Are you sure I can't help you with the dishes?" she asked Myrna, while still keeping one eye on the clock.

The older woman glanced pointedly at Letitia's manicured hands. "I don't think those long nails would appreciate your abusing them. In fact, if you're intending to finish cleaning up the house you better get yourself a good pair of rubber gloves so you don't ruin your hands."

Letitia added it to her rapidly growing list. She escaped to her bedroom with just enough time to re-brush her hair into a ponytail and spritz on her favorite scent. She hurried through the house then deliberately slowed her pace when she stepped out onto the front porch.

"Well, are you coming or not?"

She looked out and noticed the pickup truck parked in front of the house. Tyler leaned against the front fender, his arms crossed in front of his chest, one ankle cocked in front of the other. With his hat pulled down over his eyes and his dusty clothing, he looked like an advertisement for the quintessential western man.

"This man is danger with a capital D," she murmured, walking down the steps. "It's a good thing I'm well equipped."

"Oh, you're well equipped all right," Tyler drawled, his storm-colored eyes lingering on her slim figure. "The test is if your equipment can stand up to mine."

Letitia's smile broadened at his suggestive remark. "Trust me, cowboy, you're the easiest critter I've come up against in a long time. A snap." She snapped her fingers to prove it.

He straightened up and pulled open the passenger door. "I'm not as easy as you think I am, sweetheart, but I'm worth it."

Letitia looked over her shoulder. Her haughty expression rivaled anything a member of royalty could come up with. "That's *countess* sweetheart to you, slave."

Tyler grinned, pleased with her comeback. "That's what I like about you. You're willing to give as good as you get." He closed the door and walked around to the driver's side. "At this rate, you just might last longer than we thought." He started up the truck with a minimum of fuss.

"You act as if all of you set up a betting pool." She peered at him closely. There was nothing to indicate his thoughts at the moment, but still there was something in his expression that... "Wait a minute. You took bets on how long I'd stay here before I screamed in horror and ran back to the big city?"

"Ranching is a lonely business. You do what you can to relieve the monotony. And we all enjoy a good betting pool." He downshifted as they coasted over a cattle guard. "At the time, you were a perfect outlet."

Letitia flopped back in the seat. When she felt her nails dig into her palms, she consciously relaxed them. She stared intently out the window at gently rolling hills with tall mountains far off in the distance. Her imagination took off full tilt as she visualized Indians in colorful war paint overtaking the truck. Hmm, if she remembered correctly, Indians had some wonderful ways of dealing with their enemies. She wondered if she could find a book on the subject.

"How long did you give me?"

At first, Tyler pretended not to hear her question. Although, even after this short acquaintance, he should have realized that Letitia refused to be ignored.

"I hope you lost a lot of money," she said as if he'd answered her.

"Ten bucks so far. We drew up a new pool last night since you've already stayed longer than anyone figured on. I decided I'd be more conservative this time around."

She nodded her understanding. "You expected me to demand to be taken back to the airport the first day, didn't you?"

"I figured you'd want to go back within the first hour, actually," he admitted, lulled by her soft voice. "Most bet on various times the first day. One even gave you twenty-four hours," he added generously.

She fumed. "What a shame I made it so difficult for you."

"Not really. Actually, your stubbornness in facing the truth is making this pool a hell of a lot more interesting than 'Monday Night football.'"

It was a good thing Tyler didn't see Letitia's smile or he'd think he had something to worry about.

"Well, I'm glad I've been able to provide you men with so much amusement." Her tone was conversational, unthreatening. She glanced at his hands lying relaxed on the steering wheel. It was so easy to imagine him strung up by the thumbs. Then she visualized Tyler tarred and feathered. The thought was so satisfying she couldn't stop smiling as she considered other appropriate tortures she could have Tyler and the men subjected to. Each more ghastly than the last. "Perhaps I can come up with something really horrible in the near future," she murmured.

Tyler glanced at her, confused by her out-of-the-blue comment. "Excuse me?"

She continued smiling. "Not a chance."

Letitia's first glimpse of what the local residents called town was enlightening. A gas station with adjoining café, a feed store, a store that Tyler explained carried anything a body needed in a hurry, and a saddle shop that advertised boots, tack and leather goods.

"This is pretty much a stop gap for things we need," he told her, parking in front of the emporium and getting out. "There's a larger town about a two-hour drive south of here where we can do major stocking up. Every couple months a few of us drive into Butte."

Letitia was aware of curious stares as she jumped down from the truck without Tyler's help.

"Momma, why's she wearing her bedroom slippers? Did she hurt herself?" one little girl piped up, pointing at Letitia's feet.

Letitia laughed. "I guess they do look like bedroom slippers," she freely admitted, hoping to ease the mother's embarrassment as she leaned over and

shushed her daughter. "Hello, I'm Letitia DeMarco."
She smiled warmly at the woman.

"We've heard of you." The woman's smile wasn't
as warm and friendly as Letitia's.

Letitia's smile dimmed a bit.

"Afternoon, Paula," Tyler greeted the woman and
grinned at the girl. "Heather, how come you're not in
school?"

"I don't go to school til next year, Tyler, and you
know it," she answered giggling.

Tyler couldn't miss Paula's unfriendly manner toward Letitia. "How's Bret doing, Paula?"

Her manner warmed considerably when she turned
to him. "The doctor said he'll get the cast off next
week. He's real happy about that. He's always complaining that it itches all the time."

Tyler chuckled. "Yeah, I remember feeling the same
way when I broke my arm last winter. If he needs any
help, tell him to give me a call. I'm sure Mrs. DeMarco
is willing to show herself as a good neighbor and help
out any way she can."

Paula shot a doubtful glance at Letitia dressed in an
outfit that Letitia considered casual, but was the
height of fashion and sophistication to Paula.

"You really intend to work the ranch?" she asked
bluntly.

"I'm going to do my best," Letitia replied. "I asked
my brother to send me a lot of research material. He's
an author, so he understands how important research
is."

Paula shook her head and shot Tyler a look filled
with sympathy. She grasped her daughter's hand.
"Nice to meet you, Mrs. DeMarco," she said quietly,
starting to move on.

"Same here." Letitia's smile had decidedly drooped by now.

Tyler felt a tug deep down. After all, how could Letitia know that Paula only treated her that way because the young woman wasn't happy with the remote life ranching offered and probably secretly yearned after the exciting life Letitia led. And Letitia had been friendly toward her instead of acting all high-and-mighty the way he figured she would.

"Paula's always shy around people she doesn't know," he explained. "She'll warm up after she gets to know you better. You'll see."

She squared her shoulders. She'd never backed down from a battle before and she didn't intend to start doing so now. "That isn't it and we both know it. She sees me as some spoiled city girl who's here to play cowgirl until I get bored and head back for the bright lights and wild parties."

Tyler winced at her accurate description. He'd already heard some of the townspeople's speculation about the new owner of Running Springs Ranch. And none of it had been complimentary.

"You'll find out that around here, lots of people don't move around the way people elsewhere do, except from one ranch to another," he thought to explain.

Her expression told him she wasn't buying it. "I would think that would cause inbreeding over the years."

Tyler looked down. He wasn't surprised his hand was clenched in a fist that he wouldn't have minded putting through a wall. The woman did seem to enjoy trying his patience.

His jaw worked convulsively. "What I'm trying to say is that we have families who have ranched here for the past hundred, hundred-fifty years."

"Naturally, they can close ranks against any newcomers," Letitia mocked with eyes flashing. "Let me make something clear, buster. I'll be a hell of a lot better boss than Giancarlo ever was because I really care what happens here. Maybe I haven't been here long enough for people to believe me, but that's all right. I'll prove my worth by finding out what went wrong out there and by fixing it." Her eyes flashed with determination.

Tyler brushed past her and opened the door leading to the leather goods shop. Instead of holding the door open for Letitia, he walked in confident she would follow. She deliberately held back, hoping it would slap him hard on the backside. She made a face when it didn't.

She walked inside and looked around the dim interior. Her first impression was the rich scent of leather mixed with the sharper tang of leather polish. Two saddles sat on a sawhorse in one corner while an entire wall was filled with shelves of boots in various sizes and types of leather. She fingered a fancy red leather bridle studded with silver conches. The touch of the butter-soft leather intrigued her so much, she strolled around touching a bridle here, fingering a pair of moccasins there.

"Who the hell is interrupting my afternoon?" The tallest man Letitia had ever seen parted a pair of cotton curtains that shielded the rear of the shop and walked to a waist-high counter. He wore jeans and a white T-shirt smudged with leather polish. He grinned at Tyler.

"Afternoon, Tyler," he greeted then glanced curiously at her. "Considering I just sold you a pair of dress boots a month ago, I can't believe you've worn them out yet. 'Course we all know that's possible with your social life." He boomed with laughter.

Letitia's smile felt stiff on her face as she listened to the men's laughter.

"Rance, this is Letitia DeMarco of Running Springs. Mrs. DeMarco, Rance Howell, the town's resident leather artist. A pair of boots made by him is a work of art. Rance, this lady needs a pair of good work boots."

Rance walked around the counter and eyed her feet with an expert eye. He made a face at her ballet flats.

"Seven narrow?"

She blinked at his correct assumption. "Yes."

He nodded. "I've got a pair in the back that I'd made for Hazel Knott's daughter, but she changed her mind after she saw them. She decided she wanted something a lot fancier. They'd do fine although you'd be better with a pair that's custom-made for you." He looked at her under heavy brows as he demanded, "What in the hell are those things you have on your feet? Those little shoes you're wearing now ain't fit for even housework."

"Then it's a good thing I don't wear them when I do housework," she quipped. "But if I have to wear custom-made boots for that chore I might as well shoot myself."

Tyler closed his eyes. Rance was well known to take his craft seriously. More than one man had limped out of here because he'd said the wrong thing to the bootmaker.

Rance chuckled. "I heard Italians have spunk. Guess you're proof of that."

"I only married an Italian, Mr. Howell," she corrected.

"Well, I'd say you got all the fire and the looks of a genuine countess." Rance grinned, but Letitia didn't hear him, snared as she was by Tyler's eyes.

"I think I'll get those boots for you to try on." Rance was smiling broadly as he disappeared into the rear of the shop.

Neither heard him as they continued staring at each other. Letitia couldn't move as she looked into Tyler's gray eyes. How did he do it? she wondered, feeling an odd weakness invade her body. As if that wasn't bad enough, a lazy liquid heat ran through her veins. Just by looking at her, he was causing some strange feelings that her ex-husband at his most passionate never caused! She decided to put it down to the fumes from the leather polish. Yes, that was it. The fumes were like some rare exotic drug, making her feel things she ordinarily wouldn't. She'd be fine once she got outside and breathed in some fresh air.

Letitia broke the searing contact. "Well, if he's so talented why is he working here?"

"Instead of the big city where he could make boots for weekend cowboys who'd be willing to pay triple the price or more?"

She winced. "That's not what I meant and you know it, although most men with this kind of skill do tend to gravitate toward a broader market where they can command the high prices. I've heard of people paying thousands of dollars for custom-made boots."

Tyler shook his head. "Hey Rance!" he raised his voice. "Did you finish those fancy cobra-skin boots you showed me a couple weeks ago?"

"Sure did." A moment later, the man came out with a pair of boots in each hand. He held up the larger pair. "What do you think?"

Tyler took them out of his hand. He blew out a low whistle of appreciation as he studied them from all angles. "Very nice. Wish I could afford them."

Letitia braced her hand on Tyler's shoulder as she gazed over the taut cloth expanse where she could have a better look. She would freely admit to the world she knew nothing about boots, but she did know shoes and could recognize a fine craftsman.

"You are a true artist," she murmured.

Tyler remained still, acutely aware of Letitia's light touch searing him through the cloth and the scent of her skin surrounding him in a lightly perfumed cloud. What was it about her that drove him nuts? Why couldn't he ignore her the way he had other women in the past? He gritted his teeth and tried to forget about the sudden heat settling in his jeans. When he caught Rance smiling knowingly at him he glared deadly bullets at the man.

Rance named a famous country-western singer. "He's been buying my boots for the past ten years," he explained. "I keep a pattern on hand and he just calls up and tells me what he wants." He went on to name some of his other repeat clients. "I came out here fifteen years ago because I wanted to take it easy. To sit in a rocking chair on the porch and just turn into an ornery old man who likes his peace and quiet. Except it didn't work out that way." He laughed. "Instead, my old clients tracked me down and what with the folks around here not having anyone to make them a decent pair of boots, I wound up getting more work than I ever did before." He walked over to a bench and gestured Letitia to another bench across from him. "Come on, missy, let's see if these fit as well as I know they will."

She looked skeptical as she sat down and studied the gleaming black leather boots. "Are you sure these are me?"

"I think the lady is more used to those fancy polished English riding boots than a good pair of western ones, Rance," Tyler spoke up.

She looked horrified. "Have you ever worn jodhpurs? Let me tell you, you can't gain one ounce while wearing them. Not to mention they flare out at the sides like wings that make your hips look huge! And as far as I'm concerned, they look just plain silly. And that riding English-style may be accepted in parts of the world, but that doesn't mean you have to like it. Rising up and down in the saddle just the right way and nothing to grab on to if you start to fall off. Oh please!" She gave an unladylike snort.

"She's head and shoulders over that other guy who owned the ranch, Tyler." Rance grinned.

"She can't even ride," he informed him.

"I told you, I can ride. I just can't ride very well and I'm not very fond of horses," she argued. "And I never rode using a western saddle."

"Don't worry, you'll learn soon enough." Rance held up one of the boots. "Now let's get you out of those little scraps of leather shoes and into a pair of real footwear."

Letitia slipped off her shoes and extended her feet so Rance could put the boots on. He then instructed her to stand up and stamp her foot several times.

"I'm sure she'll have no problem doing that," Tyler observed.

Letitia shot him a look fit to kill before standing up and setting each foot down with a decided thump as if squashing a bug. She walked around the store a few times.

"They're very comfortable."

Rance laughed at the surprise in her voice. "They're the only kind to have. When a man's working long hours on his feet he needs boots that won't hurt and he doesn't want to suffer blisters until he can get them broken in. You don't get any blisters in boots I make. They're so comfortable you'd be convinced a lover is holding your feet when you wear them."

"Somehow, when I imagine my foot being massaged, I'd like to think of something a bit more human doing the job," she said archly.

Tyler's attention immediately directed itself on her feet. "Hmm. I'll see what can be arranged."

"I still say you need a pair custom-made for your feet, but these'll hold you over until I get a pair made up," Rance told her, confident she'd be buying and ordering, which she did.

Before Letitia left the shop, a pattern of her feet had been made and her new boots were in a box tucked under Tyler's arm.

Tyler glanced down at his watch. "I better pick up the supplies or Myrna will have my hide."

"Tyler." She laid her hand on his arm before he could move away from her. "Thank you for bullying me into buying the boots. You're right, they will work better on the ranch."

"I doubt anyone could bully you and live to tell the day," he commented sardonically.

"You did, sort of. Sometimes that's what I need." She waited while he stowed the box in the back of the truck. "At least, that's what my brother says. But then, he's a brother and what does he know?"

He recalled the feel of her hand on his shoulder. "His knowledge probably comes from years of experience dealing with you," he breathed, feeling the potent force of her guileless charm, even at this short distance. He made a quick vow to stay out of her way as much as possible. But he already knew that wouldn't be as easy as he'd like. "Come on, there's more to do."

Letitia's eyes shone with excitement as she followed Tyler into the two-story clapboard building whimsically labeled Town Emporium.

"Afternoon, Ezra," Tyler greeted a gray-haired man who was filling a box with groceries.

"Tyler." His eyes betrayed frank curiosity as they skimmed over Letitia.

"Hello." She greeted him with a broad smile as she walked up to him with her hand outstretched. "I'm Letitia DeMarco."

"You're that Eyetalian lady who now owns Running Springs." He pronounced it as if it was a fatal disease.

"Maybe you should consider using your maiden name, countess. It might give you a better reception," Tyler murmured in her ear as he walked past, then raised his voice. "Letitia, this is Ezra Murdock. He's run the store since he took it over in nineteen fifty-two. We wouldn't know what to do without him having the basics for us."

She steadfastly ignored Tyler while keeping her gaze on Ezra. "You have a fascinating establishment here." She continued to concentrate on the scowling Ezra. "It's wonderful a person can find anything they want in one place."

"People 'round here don't have time to make half-day drives just to buy somethin'," he mumbled, continuing to fill the box. He looked past her. "You here to pick up Myrna's order, Tyler?"

"That's right," he replied, handing the older man a sheet of paper. "She said she also needs these."

Ezra nodded as he scanned the list. "No problem. I'll have them out in a jiffy."

"I thought westerners were friendly to newcomers," Letitia said softly once Ezra was out of earshot. "So far, I'm not having any luck."

"You're city folk and still suspect."

She eyed a cast-iron frying pan hanging from a hook on the wall and instantly discarded her notion. With her luck, she'd only dent a perfectly good pan on his perfectly hard head. She stalked off before she could reconsider.

Tyler shook his head as he watched her walk away. "Damn, why does she do this to me?"

"Have to admit she's easy on the eyes." Ezra walked out, carrying a fifty-pound bag of flour. Tyler moved forward to help. It was a known fact the elderly man resisted anyone thinking he couldn't carry heavy items, but he was also smart enough not to turn down sincere offers of help. "Is she trying to frilly up the place with lace and chintz yet?"

Tyler shook his head. He found his attention distracted by the musical sound of Letitia's humming as she poked her way around the store with genuine interest, each new discovery she made lighting up her face. "So far, she's kept out of my way. We'll have to see."

Ezra's leathery face creased in a grin. "I heard there was a bet goin' on how long she'd last."

"So far, we've had to re-bet thirteen times. The board we used ran out of space, so we had to draw up a new one," Tyler confessed.

"She looks too frail for life out here. If nothin' else, winter will get her." Ezra bobbed his head in agreement with his own words. "Yep, you can see she's a lady made for fancy parties, not ranch life. Look at those soft hands and even softer skin. She's not made for the life out here. She's for champagne and caviar. She won't like it once the heavy snows hit."

Tyler raised his hand to cover up his laughter. Ezra was proud of the fact he hadn't gone more than fifty miles from home his entire sixty-eight years on earth. His idea of fancy parties was taken from watching "Lifestyles of the Rich and Famous" or whatever else his television's satellite found for him.

"Excuse me, what is this?" Letitia held up a strange-looking contraption.

Ezra shot Tyler a look as if to say, "See, she doesn't even know simple kitchen aids." He hitched up his suspenders. "That there's an apple corer."

"Oh," she breathed. "I'll have to have Myrna show me exactly how it works," she declared, setting it down in the bin she first found it resting in. "This store is full of all these wonderful gadgets I never knew existed. I admit I'm a novice to this way of life, but I intend to learn."

Ezra snorted as he went in the back for another sack of flour. "Women are meant to keep the house and have the babies."

"Men say that because they know that *they'd* never last through the morning sickness stage. And as for labor..." Letitia rolled her eyes in dramatic fashion. "...they'd probably ask for the painkillers the minute the first real contraction hit."

Tyler grasped her arm with a none too gentle grip. "All right, enough," he said quietly, hustling her out of the store with quick dispatch. "We've done a lot of business with Ezra over the years and I don't want to ruin that relationship now."

"Cowboys are chauvinists," she accused.

"Yeah, well, that's what makes us happy." He unlocked the truck door and pushed her inside. "You stay here. I'll be out in a few minutes."

She was indignant. "I'm supposed to give the orders here."

"Not right now."

Letitia swiveled around in the seat and watched Tyler use an economy of motions in loading up the truck with supplies. Another box labeled U. S. Mail was set next to the groceries.

He can lift all that and not even breathe hard, she thought, enjoying the view with frank female appreciation. With that thought came another more tantalizing reflection. Could he make love with the same energy and still breathe easily? It was a tempting thought. One she knew she'd have to keep to herself before she made the kind of mistake she couldn't correct.

Chapter Six

Couldn't that woman remain quiet for more than five seconds or wasn't it in her nature to just sit there with that sweet little mouth firmly shut?

If she wasn't chattering to him or to anyone in general, she was humming. And if she wasn't humming, she was looking as if she was bursting to release some important secret to the world. Hell, even her *thoughts* came out loud and clear!

Tyler hadn't missed her watching him while he loaded up the truck. She studied him as if he was some kind of bug under a microscope, for God's sake! He swerved to miss a pothole. His action threw Letitia hard against his shoulder.

"Sorry," she murmured, immediately straightening up. Before she could take a breath, she was thrown in the other direction. She uttered a curse under her breath when her shoulder painfully collided with the door handle.

"Sorry." This time it was Tyler's turn to apologize, although his tone was more terse than polite.

Letitia gave up trying to sit straight and settled for leaning against the door. "Are you angry with me for

something in particular or just because I happen to be
here?''

He could feel his jaw tighten. What did the lady expect? That he'd welcome her with open arms after her
taking away his best hope of getting a place of his
own? "Which answer would you prefer to hear?"

"Neither." She slipped her sunglasses down her
nose and watched him over the rims. A tiny smile
teased her lips. "But you could tell me how well I'm
doing after only two days and how you just know I'll
fit in around here in no time."

"Yeah, well, that might be tough." He spared her
a brief glance. "I always believe in telling the truth, no
matter how much it hurts."

Unperturbed, she shrugged his statement off. Deep
down, she knew he wasn't insulting her, merely stating a fact. "I'll be the first to admit a person can't
learn all about ranching in two days, but it's not as if
I already didn't know the difference between a horse
and a cow. And that the men are called hands, not just
employees. Although I will have to reconsider calling
that overgrown canine of yours a dog."

"He's half wolf."

Her eyes widened. "Wolf? Which half?" Horrify-
ing images of her beloved Le Chat chewed to bloody
bits danced before her eyes.

"The front half. You know, the half with the teeth."

"That isn't what I meant and you know it," she
huffed, leaning forward far enough to punch him in
the arm as hard as she could. She only wished she
could inflict more damage.

"Ow! Hey, watch those nails, countess." He flexed
his injured arm, lifting and raising it as if to make sure
it was still in good working order.

"And stop calling me countess." Letitia's temper was up just enough to put her in fighting mode.

"Sorry, but I can't see myself calling you Mrs. DeMarco."

"Then try Letitia," she snapped. "It's not that difficult a name."

Tyler frowned. "One thing I can't understand is why your mother would slap an old-fashioned name like that on you. What was it? Family obligation?"

The last thing she wanted to discuss was her name. "Nothing of the sort. It was to make up for a very boring last name."

He frowned as he recalled her mentioning her brother. "Montgomery is a boring name?"

Letitia shook her head. "I explained to you before that Jack and I had different fathers. My father's last name was Jones."

Tyler barked with laughter. "Jones? Letitia *Jones*?"

"There is nothing wrong with Jones," she retorted.

"No, I guess not since probably one fourth of the population has that name." Tyler shook his head. "No wonder you didn't want to take back your maiden name. No one would believe the name went with the face."

Letitia narrowed her eyes. She easily recognized his compliment on one hand and the insult on the other. "Normally, I have unlimited patience, but you are sorely trying the little I have left."

Tyler was tempted to tell her that she tried a hell of a lot more than his patience. Her light touch on his arm seemed to burn through the heavy fabric of his shirt.

"All I want to do is learn about ranching," she said softly. "Is that so wrong?"

"Damn!" Tyler roared, slapping the steering wheel with the flat of his hand. "Do you have to ask with your eyes all wide open like that? And that little tremble to your mouth?"

Letitia lightly patted her face with her fingertips, lingering around her mouth and eyes.

"Wouldn't a mirror be easier?" He couldn't help but be amused by her gestures.

"I never carry one."

"Then how do you get your lipstick on straight and all that makeup you socialites wear?" he teased.

Letitia stuck her nose up in the air. "Any proper lady can apply lipstick without a mirror and I'm never worried about anything else."

Tyler shook his head. True, why gild the lily? Was it instinct that allowed her to so effortlessly charm him when he didn't want to be charmed? He had to admit there wasn't a manipulative bone in her body. He'd met enough of that type of woman during his years traveling around before settling down at Running Springs. No, Letitia had a way that had to be categorized all her very own. A way that was turning out to be extremely dangerous to his mental health!

"I used to have a nice quiet sane life," he murmured.

Letitia grinned. My, my, she was getting to the man! "The loss of that nice quiet sane life couldn't have something to do with my arrival, could it?"

"Countess, it *all* has something to do with you."

She leaned over. She decided the least she could do was give him something to think about.

"Well then, cowboy, you should be very glad I brought some excitement into your life," she breathed against his cheek.

He could swear his skin tightened in reaction. When she pulled back, she left a soft cloud of perfume and the heated memory of the touch of her hand against his neck. Tyler wasn't sure which was worse. It didn't matter. He wouldn't have done without either one.

His fingers tightened on the curve of the steering wheel as he forced air in and out of his lungs in a normal manner. If only he could calm the raging inferno in his jeans just as easily. He felt he was having a good chance of doing just that when a faint musical sound reached his ears. She was humming again! By now, Tyler's fingers felt permanently welded to the steering wheel as he concentrated on the road ahead of him. He thought about hitting a few more potholes to catch her attention but discarded the idea. If he brought Myrna's groceries in all jumbled up he'd be eating burned steak for the next six months. A strange haze developed before his eyes. A burning sensation began at his toes and worked its way up his body. What was she doing to him? Hell, if he didn't know better he'd swear she was weaving some kind of magic spell.

Tyler's patience ran out. He jerked the steering wheel to the right so sharply, Letitia almost fell off the seat.

"What's wrong? Did we hit something? Blow out a tire?" She grabbed hold of the back of the seat to keep her balance.

Tyler stopped the truck on the side of the road and tugged the parking brake up with an iron grip. He half turned and grabbed hold of Letitia's arms. Her eyes widened as he pulled her across the seat toward him.

"You are the kind of woman who could turn a man into a raving maniac," he gritted, bringing her face close to his. "You just can't leave anything alone, can you? You have to poke and prod and hum and . . . and . . ." He ran out of words to describe what was going on in the boiling turmoil that doubled as his brain. Uttering a curse, he brought her even closer and mashed his mouth against hers in a kiss that a saner Tyler would have been ashamed to admit he'd committed. It took him a minute to realize that the lady's words weren't soft moans of compliance but curses. This time in English.

"You baboon! You masculine piece of horse manure! You arrogant slime! Who do you think you are!" Her small fists rained on his head with surprising strength.

"Dammit, Letitia!" He arched backwards to keep her at a safe distance. In the small confines of the truck cab, there wasn't very far to go. "What are you doing? Watch it, that hurts!"

Letitia's face was bright red with indignation. "What am *I* doing? What about you! You can't tell me that you don't know how to kiss a woman properly," she raged, pounding her fist downward.

Tyler winced when her fist just missed the rapidly declining bulge in his jeans. "No offense, but if you continue doing that my hope one day of having children could turn into a dream," he yelped, still stunned by her fury.

"Considering your technique, that might not be so bad," she snapped.

Letitia leaned forward until her nose bumped his. Her narrowed eyes sent aquamarine lasers through his head. "Now, cowboy, let me show you how it should be done." She placed her hands on either side of his head in such a tight grip he couldn't have moved it if he wanted to.

Letitia's breath was soft on his face as she brushed her lips against his. "Softly. See, just a teasing touch," she murmured. Her tongue darted out for a quick taste.

Tyler's head was spinning. Her perfume wove silvery webs around his senses as her kisses wove another kind of web, equally as strong, around another part of him that was more than willing to give in to her.

Letitia wasn't exactly sure when the tables turned. Only that they did with astonishing ease. Tyler's mouth was suddenly the one in charge of this kiss and the man positively knew what he was doing! Her eyes popped open, and found his watching her. She lurched drunkenly when his hand found its way under her blouse to the lace edge of her bra, and arched forward for more of his touch.

He pulled back. "Is that what you were talking about, countess?" he asked in a raspy voice that couldn't hide his arousal. Of course, if she doubted it, all she had to do was look at his lap!

Letitia opened her mouth and just as suddenly closed it again. For once in her life, she didn't know what to say.

"I—" She coughed to clear her throat but her voice still came out higher pitched than usual. "I don't think that was such a good idea."

Tyler stared at her long and hard. Hectic color now dotted her cheeks, her lips were free of lipstick but tinted a bright pink and swollen from their kiss, and her eyes were huge in her face. His thoughts could be considered chauvinistic of the first order, but right now he didn't care. If she responded so wholeheartedly to a kiss, what would have happened if they had gone further? The idea was mind-boggling! He tried to remind himself that the lady he was kissing was the enemy. And as the enemy, he should be fighting her, not trying to wrestle her onto the truck seat. Obviously, she agreed with him.

"Why?" His voice was husky, raw with memories.

"Why what?"

"Why wasn't it such a good idea?" His question was loaded with meaning. Since she started it, she could finish it.

She licked her lips as she racked her brain for a suitable answer. "Because we have to deal with each other on a day-to-day basis and this kind of incident could make it difficult," she said slowly.

Tyler felt the fury surround him. He should have known better! He stretched his arm across the back of the seat and leaned toward her. "Excuse this poor cowpoke for not knowing his place, countess," he drawled mockingly. "Working for royalty is new to me. I'll try and do better." His gaze sent the temperature plummeting to below freezing.

For the first time in her life, Letitia thought very seriously about murder. Not in the teasing way, either. She forced her gaze to meet his without wavering. Besides, if she looked lower she would see a broad bare chest that displayed a mat of sun-tipped brown hair. When had she unbuttoned his shirt? She'd kissed her share of men in her life, some more sophisticated in the art than others. Yet none of them had ever left her feeling as if she existed in another world the way Tyler did. And none of them left her feeling as if she wouldn't mind seeing them torn up into little pieces just as quickly. Not even Giancarlo and Stephano had evoked these strong emotions.

"You are the most . . ."

"Remember what happened the last time you began your little tirade?" His quietly spoken threat hit the appropriate nerve.

She hissed a curse in Italian. He was glad he didn't understand the word even if he understood the meaning. If the lady had a gun she would have shot him down.

When he put the truck in gear, the tension hovered over them like a thick fog.

BY THE TIME Tyler stopped the truck by the ranch-house back door, he felt as if he'd survived several wars. Surprisingly, Letitia hadn't let out a peep for the past twenty minutes. He'd been waiting for her next outburst with baited breath. Instead, she sat back in the seat looking out the window as if she was on a pleasure drive. While Tyler ran ideas through his mind in hope of finding a reasonable way of getting her permanently off the ranch. She didn't belong here and he intended to prove it. Having his own piece of property had been a dream for more than fifteen years now. He wasn't about to let some flighty socialite take it away from him when he'd been so close to obtaining it. Now all he had to do was convince her she was better off out of here. And that no one better deserved owning Running Springs than he did.

Sure, he knew it would be difficult. Especially since his financial picture wasn't any more solid than hers. But he did have something she didn't: the knowledge.

He just wished he had an idea what his next move should be.

As he slowed the truck he looked out the windshield with disbelief at what he saw. "What the hell?" he muttered, grabbing the door handle and climbing outside. "What's going on here?" he roared to no one in general.

Letitia scrambled out of the truck and hurried around the front. The scene in front of her dissolved any anger she'd felt earlier.

"This is too much," she bubbled.

"Too much? This is ridiculous! Duffy, what's your problem?" Tyler strode across the yard toward the large dog who was sitting under a tree with a preening Le Chat positioned between his paws. "You're a dog! You should have whipped that cat's ass that first time!"

The dog looked up and whined at the sound of his master's furious voice.

"I'd say he's trying to tell you it's better to be friends than enemies," Letitia commented from behind. "You know, make love, not war."

"That's not exactly the way I'd put it." He glared at his dog who ducked his head in guilt. "This is all your fault!" He directed his outrage toward Letitia and Le Chat. The cat looked Tyler up and down with his usual disdain. His mistress's expression was close enough to be a mirror image.

"Then how would you put it?"

Tyler spun on his heel and started to open his mouth. He held his forefinger up in the air as if making an important point. Then, as if thinking better of it, he snapped his mouth shut and stalked off. His fists opened and clenched at his sides. He clearly wanted to throttle something and he thought better of staying around Letitia for much longer.

"You seem to like to throw out challenging statements and then refuse to back them up!" Letitia shouted after him.

"Considering the man's mood the milk is probably curdled," she announced to a surprised Myrna as she breezed through the kitchen.

"I'm going to kill her," Tyler muttered, striding past J.T. who was walking up from the barn to see what all the commotion was about. "I'm going to tear her into little pieces and bury her in a field along with that damn fur ball she calls a cat."

"Before or after you make love to her?" the older man joked.

He glared at the man as if he would join Letitia. "Both."

DINNER WAS FILLED with silent speculation as both combatants were conspicuously absent.

"Tyler said he has a date," J.T. told Myrna.

"Madame filled a plate with cheese and crackers and said something about going over the paperwork," she replied.

"Never knew the boss could get so het up," Ben commented, immediately reaching for a large bowl of fluffy mashed potatoes. "Lots of things happen and he's never lost his temper like he does with her."

Myrna rapped his knuckles with a serving spoon. "Are you men already talking about them?"

The young man looked up and realized the mistake he'd made could cost him second helpings. "Not really," he stammered. "I mean, she's only been here a couple days and . . ." He shrugged helplessly.

The older woman stood at the head of the table with her arms crossed in front of her chest. She slowly scanned each face. "We all expected changes around here with the new owner. I'm one of the most obstinate people the good Lord put on this earth. If I'm willing to give her a chance, you should too."

"Why should you want to give her a chance? You don't really know her," one of the hands commented.

"She didn't complain about having to clean house without any help." She clearly felt that said it all.

LETITIA SAT CROSS-LEGGED in the middle of the bed with various sheets of paper surrounding her. She'd begun the tedious task of sorting out papers into additional piles from the piles she'd already begun. Le Chat lay curled up in the rocking chair, which now sported a clean blue floral cushion that Letitia suspected Myrna had put there. She shifted her position each time her stomach rumbled.

"You were stupid to remain in here," she mumbled to herself, studying a receipt for a used Studebaker. It was dropped on the throwaway pile after she exclaimed over the price a car had once cost.

"Land sakes, girl, it's a lovely night. You shouldn't be in here. You should be outside."

Myrna stood in the doorway holding a plate. The enticing aroma tempted Letitia's stomach to growl loud and strong.

"I knew you were just being stubborn." The older woman pulled a small table next to the bed and set the plate on it. She picked up Le Chat and deposited him on the floor before settling in the rocking chair. The cat immediately jumped back into the chair and curled up on her lap. "Damn cat," she groused.

Letitia grinned. "He doesn't do that just for anyone. Usually he sharpens his claws on people's legs."

"He wasn't in for dinner, either."

She concentrated on her food. She wasn't going to pretend to misunderstand who Myrna was talking about. "Oh? Was he pouting?"

"If you mean acting like you, maybe. He also had a date."

She continued eating as if the news didn't surprise her, even though it was very unwelcome to her ears. "Even ranch foremen are entitled to evenings off."

Myrna hid her smile. Letitia wasn't as unconcerned as she pretended to be. "Tell me something and tell me straight. What exactly do you want here? What do you hope will happen?"

Letitia forked up a tender green bean and chewed it reflectively. "I want to learn to be my own person. To not have to depend on anyone but myself. To prove I can do something other than plan parties and play tennis, which I hate by the way."

Myrna was surprised by her candid reply. "Are you always this honest with your feelings?"

She nodded. "I decided a long time ago I wasn't going to hold back my views just in case someone didn't like what I was going to say. Oh, I don't mean saying hurtful things, but I don't see anything wrong in speaking out."

Myrna nodded. "Is it because of your ex-husband that you don't want to depend on anyone?"

She shrugged. "Partly. You see, my mother took wonderful care of my brother and me between her marriages. You would think she was one of the most self-sufficient people around, even if her sense of direction was the worst and we never spent a holiday where we planned to. But once she got married, she was one of the most dependent persons you could ever meet. She expected her husband to take care of everything for her. I didn't mean to, but when I married Stephano I acted like that because he expected his wife to be that way and because I felt I was supposed to. Well, I grew up and he didn't." She grimaced. "He thought life revolved around polo and other women. I felt there should be more to it, so I left him and ran to my brother. Except all I did was become dependent on *him*. Oh, I made talk about traveling and all, but that's all it was—talk. Then Jack got married and I knew it was time to let him go on with his life and for me to find mine," she murmured.

"And you found it with Giancarlo?" Skepticism colored the cook's voice.

Letitia wrinkled her nose. "Yes, well, we all make mistakes and he was a major one for me. And, as far as I'm concerned, my last one. I don't know why, but Italian men fascinated me since the first time Mother took us to Italy. I was fourteen and this mature seventeen-year-old boy gave me my first kiss. After that, I was a sucker for big brown eyes."

"And now?"

"And now, I can't even stand Italian food."

Myrna chuckled.

Letitia scooted back until she rested against the pillows. "Why are you out here?"

"I've been cooking for Running Springs since my husband brought me here as a bride more than thirty years ago," she explained, adding matter-of-factly, "He was killed eight years ago when he was trampled by a bronc. Neither of us had any family other than each other, so I just stayed on."

Letitia watched Myrna's hands caress Le Chat's back in long slow strokes. The older woman's hands showed her age from all her hard work over the years, but Le Chat didn't seem to care as he purred contentedly under her attention. "I didn't think you were fond of cats."

"This one is different. He's got quite a personality."

"Some would say too much," she said dryly.

"He's sure got that dog of Tyler's snowed."

Letitia joined in. "I could see that, but I don't think it makes Tyler very happy."

"He's a man who feels cats should be afraid of dogs. Your cat took that theory and tossed it out the window."

Letitia looked down at her crossed ankles. She wiggled her toes, idly noticing it was time for a pedicure. "If the ranch is doing so badly, how are the groceries paid for and other staples needed around here? Or does Tyler make sure there's enough for that?"

She looked at her sharply. "Tyler does the best he can with what he has. The ranch does have some income, just not as much as it needs to make a real go of itself. To help out, some of us have even taken pay cuts. But if you want to know how it works, you'll have to talk to Tyler."

Letitia wasn't looking forward to that.

"Myrna, do you think I can make a go of it?"

"Of showing the hands you've got staying power or doing something positive with the ranch?"

"Both."

The older woman thought for a moment. "Depends on how much grit you've got. I already have an idea you're pretty stubborn. You'll need that and more to deal with the bank about the quarterly loan payment that's late."

"Oh, banks!" Letitia waved her hand around in an airy dismissal. "Bankers love me," she confided. "They're like old softies around me. They treat me like their long lost granddaughter and give me anything I need, if not more. I read the paperwork on the loan and I can handle it." She didn't bother saying that the quarterly payments were much more than she expected. And for the moment, she wasn't sure how she was going to come up with the money.

"You'll change your opinion after you meet ours," Myrna said dryly.

"He can't be that bad," she argued, albeit feebly.

"Bad? You're going to find out soon enough when you see him about the loan you're now probably liable for. Honey, our banker makes Scrooge look like a spendthrift."

Letitia didn't even think to swear in Italian this time.

Chapter Seven

He wondered if she was naked. He hated himself for even thinking it.

Tyler stood at one of the bunkhouse windows looking out. He stood there smoking a cigarette and wishing he wasn't doing either because they were both addictions he didn't need. Late one night when he couldn't sleep he'd wandered from his set of rooms and ended up downstairs. During his nocturnal search for sanity, he glanced out a window and discovered another way for Letitia to unknowingly destroy his peace of mind. All he had to do was stand at that particular window and he had a clear view of the master bedroom in the main house. Actually, it was the master-bedroom window he had a clear view of. A shade and lace curtains kept him from seeing the room's occupant. He tried to tell himself that for his mental health he was better off not seeing anything. So why was he standing up here looking over there? Again.

"I thought you quit those."

"I thought I did too." Tyler didn't turn around. "What are you doing up?"

J.T. ambled over beside him. "The older you get the less sleep you need. 'Sides, Ray is snorin' up a storm. How the others can sleep with all that noise, I don't know. He sounds like one of those damn steam engines. The night he starts whistling I'm gonna shoot him." He followed the direction of Tyler's gaze. "Son, you've got it bad. Why don't you just crawl to her window and let out a good howl? Maybe she'll take pity on you and let you come inside."

The mental picture had great possibilities. Tyler's chuckle was that of a man in pain. "J.T., you're a sick old man."

"More like a smart one. The boys are thinkin' they may as well forget drawing up a new pool. She's been here for a little over a week and hasn't said one word about leaving. She's even workin' on gettin' the house clean. I heard she's talkin' about paintin' it too. You don't do that unless you intend to stay."

Tyler sighed as he took another drag on his cigarette. The acrid smoke burned his lungs and left a horrible taste in his mouth, but he didn't care. He welcomed the discomfort because it kept his mind off the discomfort in his jeans. He wished he could blame her for all of it.

"You'd think she would have finally realized she doesn't belong here," he mumbled.

"And she wants to put in a flower garden."

Tyler was determined to remain silent on that point. It didn't last long. "Crazy woman thinking she can do all that on next to nothing," he muttered.

J.T. watched him closely. "She figures it won't be all that difficult."

"She sometimes acts like she doesn't have a brain in her head," he gritted, walking across the room to the pool table. He stubbed out his cigarette with a vicious twist in the ashtray on the edge of the pool table. "She prances around here with that sassy tail of hers twitching in the air thinkin' we're all going to do her bidding like a bunch of damn cattle. And you know what, we do! This should have been *mine*, not hers! What she knows about ranching wouldn't even fill up a thimble."

"Now, Tyler, you know very well she isn't that way," the older man gently chided. "She's never tried to push her ideas on you. And she's left you to do your job."

"Thank God," he growled. "Still, it shouldn't be my job. It should be my future." He could feel the acid burning in his gut.

"For some reason it wasn't meant to be, Tyler," J.T. said gently. "You have to let it go."

His jaw tightened. "No, I don't. All she has to do is realize she doesn't belong here and be willing to sell me the ranch at a fair price. She's broke, you'd think she'd want the money for the life she's used to."

J.T. hid his grin. He wondered if Tyler realized how frustrated he was. While Tyler's indignation was natural, there was more to it than just anger over losing his shot at the ranch. J.T would bet he was also angry because the usurper was not only a woman, but a beautiful one who was tying Tyler up in knots. He wondered what would happen if he stirred up a little turmoil. "There's some who get hitched to get a piece of land."

Tyler's gaze sliced through him like a hot knife. "I suggest you lose that idea right away," he said with deadly calm.

"Yeah, well, it isn't somethin' you should ignore.
Look on the bright side. She's a beauty. Sure wouldn't
be all that difficult to climb into bed with her, would
it?" J.T. smothered a fake yawn. "Guess I'll get back
to bed before it's time to get up. Too bad you gave up
your house."

As foreman, Tyler had the use of a small house but
had given it up when one of the hands recently got
married. He'd moved back into the bunkhouse until
they had enough free time to build a new house.

Tyler eyed him suspiciously. Why was the man
putting all these ideas in his head? "Why is it too
bad?"

J.T.'s grin was pure lechery. "It would have been
easier to sneak out of, that's why. Here, you've got too
many guys to sneak past. 'Course, you could consider it a challenge if you sneak out and back in without anyone catching you."

His jaw tightened. "I have no reason to sneak past
anyone."

The older man ignored his warning tone. "Still, you
never know when you might have a reason, what with
the way a man's blood can heat up and all. Well, good
night." He slowly made his way up the stairs. He decided he'd left Tyler more than enough to chew on.

Tyler spun on his heel until he faced the infamous
window again. He swore under his breath and then
followed J.T. back upstairs. But there was no sleep for
him for the rest of the night. As far as he was concerned, that was all right. Not sleeping meant he didn't
dream about her. And the dreams he wove in his mind
were becoming just as dangerous to his well-being as
every sight of her in the strong light of day.

JUST AS TYLER WAS ABOUT to mount his horse, a dark blue truck pulled to a stop in front of the barn.

"Hey, Tyler, got some packages for your boss." A stocky silver-haired man called out as he stepped out of the truck cab.

Tyler walked over and glanced in the back of the truck where large boxes filled the truck's bed. "Which box is hers?"

He chuckled. "All of them. Farley asked if I'd bring them out."

Tyler called over several of the men and in no time, the truck was emptied.

"When you get mail, countess, you get mail," Tyler said wryly when Letitia walked outside to see what the commotion was. "Letitia DeMarco, Wyatt Burns. He owns the next ranch over."

Letitia smiled and offered her hand. Wyatt gulped and rapidly wiped his hand on his jeans before accepting hers.

"Pleased, ma'am," he muttered.

"Thank you for being so kind to drop the boxes off," she said. "My brother said he was sending out a few things. I had no idea he'd go this far." She inspected the boxes with the eagerness of a little girl. "Can we take them inside?"

"You're the boss."

Letitia turned to Wyatt. "Would you like to come in for some coffee, Mr. Burns? It's the least I can do as a thank-you for your dropping these off."

"No, thank you." He bobbed his head in a shy manner. "Got a lot of work to do. It's a pleasure to meet you." He almost tripped getting back into his truck.

Letitia turned her attention to the many boxes.

"I guess you'll want the ones marked TV and VCR to go into the living room," Tyler commented, after directing the men. He turned around to pick up one box and grunted with effort. "Jeez, what the hell's in here?"

She glanced at the side. "It's marked books."

"It must be this year's encyclopedia," he muttered, calling one of the men over to help him.

She shrugged. "I have no idea what the others are. When I talked to Jack a few days ago, he only said he'd sent out some things I requested along with some surprises, but I couldn't imagine it would be all this," she murmured, following him inside. She deliberately hung back a few paces so she could admire the shifting muscles in Tyler's back as he helped carry in the box holding a television set. There was something about the way that man walked that stirred things up inside her!

In the end, they piled all the boxes in the living room where Letitia could easily sort everything out. While she unpacked boxes and marveled over the contents, Tyler and one of the other men set up the television set and hooked up the video tape recorder with a minimum of fuss and cussing. Letitia laughed softly as she listened to the two men amiably argue how it should be done. When she found a envelope with her name scrawled across the front, she couldn't resist opening it right away.

"Pretty fancy equipment," he commented, playing with the TV remote control. "Thing is, TV reception is pretty lousy out here. You'll be lucky if you get anything more than a lot of static."

Letitia was engrossed in reading an enclosed letter from her brother. "He says a satellite dish will be delivered in another week or so," she said in dismay. "I didn't ask for all this."

"Then you have a pretty generous brother." Tyler set down the remote control. "Anything more you need lifted?"

She shook her head. "No, everything else is very light, but thank you."

He looked at her, wondering how she could always appear so fresh. And how a woman wearing navy walking shorts and a fuschia top that heightened her light tan could look so sexy. Along with another damn pair of those little ballet slippers! He glared at the cat who strolled by wearing a collar in the same fuschia color.

"Letitia," he said huskily without even being aware he'd said her name.

She looked up, silently questioning him. He could only study her eyes, her flushed cheeks and mouth bare of lipstick. She wore little makeup and didn't seem to mind that people saw her without her mascara and lipstick on. But then, he considered her beautiful even without all the paint.

He shook his head. "Nothing." He grabbed his hat off one of the pegs by the door and walked outside.

Letitia hurried to the window where she could watch him walk back to the barn. "What was he going to say?" she mused. "And if he said something I wanted to hear, what would I have said back?"

She returned to her task of emptying the boxes, but some of the joy in unwrapping them had faded. She opened a note from her sister-in-law.

I can only assume you don't have enough casual clothing so I thought I'd include a few things I'm sure you can use.

                                        Love,
                                        Holly

Letitia held up pairs of jeans, cotton shirts with matching bandanas, several pair of running shoes and even several western-styled full skirts and tops. "Holly, you are a dear," she murmured with soft laughter as she held up matching cat collars and a box filled with several bottles of sun block. "You do think of everything."

"What do you intend to do with all that?" Myrna stood in the living-room doorway.

"These are going to help me learn about the western way of life." Letitia pointed at the television set and then at a box filled with books and video tapes.

Myrna gave in to her curiosity and rummaged through the books and tapes. "You think these will help?" Her voice was muffled as she studied the back cover of one video tape.

"They'll at least give me an idea," Letitia explained.

The older woman kept her features carefully masked. "I'll have to make sure to get a front seat to this turn of events," she muttered, walking out of the room. "Hell, maybe I'll even sell tickets."

"What's wrong?" Letitia called after her.

"You still want to learn to cook?"

Letitia's face lit up. She'd been begging Myrna for the past week to teach her culinary basics and the cook kept putting her off.

She jumped to her feet. "Of course I do!"

"Then be in the kitchen in a half hour dressed grubby. Cooking can get as dirty as working outside."

"I can't imagine that," Letitia commented, gathering up a pile of clothing and carrying it into her room. "Cooking is just adding things to a pan and making sure it doesn't burn, that's all. No big deal."

"I THOUGHT COOKING was just putting things in a pan and making sure it didn't burn." Letitia wiped the back of her hand across her forehead. She had no idea she left a streak of flour behind. "Why am I doing this?"

Myrna looked over Letitia's shoulder. "Before you can advance to cooking, you need to learn the basics."

"*Knead* is most definitely the word." She grimaced at the dough collecting under her nails. "Is there a particular reason why you chose today to bake bread? And why you bestowed this honor on me?"

She smiled benevolently. "It's nice to have help with this chore. It's time-consuming and besides, kneading bread dough is an art that should be learned early."

"I guess I'm more entertaining than the radio." Letitia paused as Myrna sprinkled a bit more flour over the dough.

"Use a lighter touch," she advised, moving off.

She glanced at the wall clock. "What about meals?"

"I always keep plenty of stews and casseroles in the freezer that just need heating for days like this," she explained, gesturing toward two large pots simmering on the stove. She proceeded to show Letitia how to divide the dough and shape it into loaves for baking. The moment the pans were placed in the oven, Letitia collapsed in a chair and drank a glass of water without pausing for a breath.

"I don't know how you do this day after day," she gasped, once she refilled her glass and sipped it more slowly.

"If I'm lucky, I only need to bake bread once a week." Myrna checked the pots and stirred the contents.

"Going to the store and buying it is much easier."

"But not as enjoyable nor as cheap."

Letitia lifted her arms and rotated her shoulders. She winced as sore muscles made themselves known. "You're used to this, I'm not."

Myrna's chuckle had Letitia grimacing. "You wanted to learn how to cook. You have to start with the basics."

"Cook, yes. Build up my arm muscles, no." She crooked one arm behind her head and slipped the other one behind her back, using the lower hand to pull the upper one down in hopes of easing her tight muscles.

"I'll show you how to cut up vegetables for a salad next."

"This sounds more like servitude than a cooking class."

"You have to start out somewhere."

"I think I'd rather muck out stalls."

"Good, you can start tomorrow." Tyler walked into the kitchen.

"Oh joy, I am *so* fortunate." She tilted her head back so she could see him and stuck her tongue out.

"Be careful with that cute pink tongue, countess." His breath was warm in her ear as his fingers pressed into her shoulders. "Or I might decide to show you what constructive things you can do with it."

The kitchen was hot enough with the ovens blasting away, but Letitia swore the room temperature soared another fifty degrees after Tyler's provocative remark sent zingers straight through her nervous system.

"You appear to have your mind on only one thing," she said softly, resisting the urge to fan her overheated face.

"It might have something to do with the source."

Letitia felt his hands leave her shoulders and the heat of his body disappear from her back when Tyler moved off to say something to Myrna. His words to the cook were nothing more than white noise in her ears as she stared at his back. A back covered in blue chambray that had a large patch of sweat in the middle. A back that was *almost* as good as the front. As if sensing her eyes on him, he turned his head and grinned. Then, as if divining her thoughts wasn't bad enough, he winked. It took a lot of effort on her part, but she made sure not to stick her tongue out again.

"Here, you can peel these." Myrna set vegetables on the counter by the sink.

Letitia flashed Tyler an audacious smile as she walked toward the sink with a hip-swinging walk she hoped raised his blood pressure good and high.

"Now what?" Myrna muttered as the telephone rang. She wiped her hands on her apron and reached for the receiver.

"Betty, how are you? Yes, I have that recipe right here. No, you use two cups sugar, not one and a half." She carried the phone over to the shelves holding her cookbooks and plucked one down, rapidly thumbing through the pages.

Letitia looked over and made sure Myrna's back was turned before silently gaining Tyler's attention. He grinned and leaned back against the counter with his arms crossed in front of his chest. He cocked an eyebrow, sending her a silent dare.

Go ahead, countess, give it your best shot.

Letitia used the smile that once charmed Omar Sharif at a garden party. She half turned and picked up a carrot from the bunch lying on the counter, slowly running her fingers down the orange vegetable. Tyler straightened up, his hands hanging at his sides. She lazily ran her tongue over her upper lip then across her lower one. His hot gaze was instantly glued to her mouth. Half turning away, she ran warm water over the carrot, brushing the excess droplets off with her fingertips. Tyler's features tightened with reaction. He lifted the glass he'd filled with water to his mouth and slowly drank the liquid. He didn't take his eyes off her once.

Letitia turned off the water and while making sure Tyler's gaze was fastened on that hand, she stealthily picked up the vegetable peeler with the other. After ensuring he was focused on what she was doing, she dug the peeler deep into the tip of the carrot and sliced upward with the skillful precision of a surgeon.

Tyler immediately choked, spewing water everywhere.

"What happened with you?" Myrna had hung up the phone and turned when Tyler began choking.

"Nothing," he wheezed, blindly setting the glass on the counter. It was pure luck he accomplished it. "I guess it went down the wrong way."

"You have to be careful with things like that," Letitia pointed out with ultra-feminine innocence as she picked up another carrot. "You could seriously hurt yourself."

He stared at her as if wondering whether to kill her fast or draw the torture out. And she stared right back, sending the tension level skyrocketing.

"Tyler?" Letitia was the first one to break the charged silence.

He continued just looking at her.

She held up one hand holding the peeled carrot, although it looked like a shiny red apple to him. The apple of temptation. "Would you like a carrot?"

He didn't bother answering as he turned and walked out the door.

"Now, don't that beat all?" Myrna frowned at the foreman's retreating figure. "Wonder what got into him? And turning down a carrot. He used to eat them the way some eat potato chips. For a while, the men called him Bugs Bunny."

Letitia shrugged as she braced her hip against the counter edge. She bit into the carrot, trying to ignore the stampeding horses in her chest. "Beats me. Men can act so strange at times, can't they?"

Chapter Eight

"Gee, countess, I'm surprised you're not luxuriating in front of your new television set watching one of the many video tapes your brother sent you."

Letitia, who'd been sitting on the top step gazing up at the sky, looked over her shoulder to greet her visitor.

"What? And be cooped up inside on a night like this?" She held her arms out. "This is so much better than anything you can find on television. The sky is clear, the stars are bright, what more can a person ask for?" She patted the wood beside her. "Have a seat."

Tyler sat down, his hip comfortably nudging hers.

"You missed a good supper," Letitia said conversationally. "Or did you have a hot date?"

"No, just had a lot of things to do. I wasn't very hungry and the truck needed the spark plugs changed, so I figured it was a good time to work on it." He inspected his hands rather than look at her. She looked like a prairie angel in a ruffled chambray skirt and a white off-the-shoulder lace top. Her hair was pulled back from her face with two combs holding the loose curls he itched to run his fingers through.

"Too bad you missed dinner. Myrna made a wonderful carrot salad." She slanted a sly glance in his direction.

He winced and shifted his weight on the boards. "I don't think so."

Letitia bit her lip to keep from bursting out laughing. She was enjoying the thought that she'd unnerved him.

"Do you get a lot of beautiful nights like this out here?" she murmured, drawing her knees up and wrapping her arms around them.

"Guess I never noticed," he admitted. "Though during the winter the snows are too high to worry about what the nights are. There's times we can't get too far, even on horseback, although for the cattle's sake, we have to do what we can. We usually bring them in closer to the ranch house then. We can get snowed in for weeks at a time." He shot her a sideways glance.

"That would be a good time to catch up on my reading," she said unperturbed. She wasn't going to allow him to bother her! "Still, you should appreciate what you have now." She drew in a lung-expanding breath of air. Tyler couldn't keep his eyes off her breasts that seemed to grow fuller with each breath she took. "It used to be I'd go outside at night and couldn't see the sky without streetlights obscuring the beauty or have the sound of cars drowning out the night sounds. This is so peaceful." Her voice was hushed. "No wonder people don't want to leave here. Here, you can feel life all around you without that frantic dash to get to the office on time or get to that client. City dwellers don't know what they're missing." She slanted him a look. A little voice inside prompted her to go further. "Especially the bigger-than-life men."

Tyler leaned across the post with one leg drawn up. "Bigger than life, huh?" The idea fascinated him. Just as she did. At the same time, he felt a sinking feeling. She truly was falling in love with the place.

She nodded. "As big as you can get. And don't let that inflate your ego too much or I'll just have to get out that pin and pop it," she teased. "We don't want everyone to think you cowboys think too much of yourselves, do we?"

He grinned. "Yeah and you would, wouldn't you?"

"But of course," she affected an accent she thought a countess would have. "Ve vill show the vorld vhat vonderful men the American vest has." She burst out giggling. "That's something I can't keep up for very long without laughing. I always feel as if I should be dressed in a forties-style dress and waiting for Humphrey Bogart to walk in and rescue me from Claude Raines."

"For a woman who's lived most of her life in Europe, you're pretty well informed about old American movies."

"Cable television helped me catch up on a lot of what I missed," she explained. "I considered it a learning experience."

Tyler leaned forward. "What all did you learn?"

His husky voice caressed her nerve endings. "Oh, a lot of things," she drew each word out with deliberate coyness.

He leaned forward even more. He could feel her sweet breath on his face. "Such as?"

She tipped her head back. "Solutions to the mysteries of life," she whispered, even though there was no one within earshot. "The right way to do certain things. And keep certain people happy."

He kept his gaze on her mouth, fascinated by the way it moved with each word she uttered. He wanted to follow those movements with his own mouth. He wanted to reacquaint himself with her taste. "Would you share those mysteries with me?"

Letitia's lips curved. "What would you like to know?"

Her perfume wove seductive patterns around him as he touched his mouth to hers. "Whatever you care to tell me." His tongue stroked her lower lip.

Her tongue darted out to touch his. "Well, there was one thing that really drove me crazy," she murmured.

Tyler's hands circled her waist. He could feel the slip and slide of silk under her blouse. "Too bad I took down that porch swing last fall and didn't bother putting it back up," he muttered.

"Why?"

"Because then we could have been a hell of a lot more comfortable than sitting here in danger of falling down these steps," he groused, unable to stop himself from pulling her into his lap. Her full skirt fell over his legs in graceful folds. She looped her arms around his neck. "I thought you fixed that broken step."

"I did, but that doesn't mean something couldn't cause us to fall off."

"Such as?" She enjoyed studying his face in the darkness that blessedly hid them from an unwanted audience.

He wasn't about to wait much longer. Having Letitia in his arms was too much temptation. "Such as this." His mouth slanted firmly over hers with his tongue plunging inward. Letitia's soft moan was just the response he wanted. He tightened his hold on her and leaned back against the post.

"Letitia, you are something out of a dream," he breathed, burying his face against the soft curve of her throat. He nipped the tender skin.

"I thought you would say a nightmare."

"That too."

She combed her fingers through his hair. "You have such silky hair. Too bad you have to wear a hat. It's nice to run my fingers through it."

His shoulders shook with laughter. "Do me a favor and don't let that piece of information get out."

She pressed her hand against the V-shaped bare skin revealed by the open collar of his shirt. "Your skin is so warm," she whispered in wonderment.

"I'm better than an electric blanket in the winter." He nuzzled his way up to her ear. "Care to find out?"

"It's not winter."

"We can pretend."

As far as Letitia was concerned, the last thing she wanted to do was pretend. Not when she sat in the very masculine lap of the real thing and could feel his arousal. She closed her eyes, allowing the sensations Tyler caused to wash over her.

"I had no idea cowboys were so...so..." She couldn't find the words to describe what he was doing to her. She only knew she didn't want him to stop.

Tyler slipped one hand under her blouse and upward. He hissed a sharp curse when he discovered she wasn't wearing a bra, only a silk camisole. Her nipple hardened to a tiny nub under his touch. He rolled it gently between his fingertips.

"Tyler." She could only whisper his name. "You're not like anyone I've met before."

"Then we're even," she murmured, entranced with the way his hair flowed between her fingers.

"You're a very dangerous lady, countess." His voice had grown raw with need.

For once, she didn't mind the nickname. "Just shut up, cowboy, and kiss me."

That was one order Tyler didn't mind following. He covered her mouth with his, drawing her into a sensual vortex that swept away all rational thought. Her skin seemed to flow like liquid silk under his fingers as he pulled her blouse from her skirt.

"This is not a good place for this," he gasped, pulling away from her. "Anyone could walk up and we wouldn't hear them until it was too late."

She laughed softly. She rested her forehead against his. "We could explain we got bored talking about television."

"The last thing you'll ever be is boring," he rasped.

She pressed a butterfly-light kiss against the corner of his eye. "So do you want me to tell you what I learned from American television?" she cooed as she continued her teasing kisses.

He grinned. He could understand this audacious Letitia the best. "Yeah."

Letitia ran the back of her fingers across his jawline and down his throat. She ran her tongue across her lips. "The most important thing I feel I learned was—" she breathed a kiss against his mouth "—who shot J.R."

Tyler's hands had tightened on her waist as she teased him with her whisper-soft kisses and wiggles that were more than enough to make him nuts. How she could take him to that brink of sensual electricity then throw him back to the bowels of sanity, he had no idea.

"You little witch," he murmured chuckling.

"No, that's my sister-in-law's job." Letitia pushed herself out of his lap and stood up. She held a hand out.

Tyler knew there was no way her slight weight could handle him, but he accepted her helping hand as he got to his feet. He immediately drew her back into his arms.

"You're a temptress, Letitia DeMarco," he told her, feeling the sparks of jealousy as he wondered just how she used this part of her nature. "Is this how you enticed Giancarlo into signing the ranch over to you? By offering your sweet mouth and promising him even more? Or had you already given it to him and he happily signed it over?"

Letitia's eyes narrowed. "So you'd like to know how I talked Giancarlo into signing the ranch over?" Her voice was pure silk.

He didn't notice the danger signals. Probably because he hated himself for even thinking such a thing, much less saying it out loud and for some crazy reason, unable to stop saying so. "Yes, I would."

She stepped back a pace. "It wasn't all that difficult. We conducted a very adult conversation after I pulled a .38 on him. I've always felt a man won't lie if a gun is aimed at him. He immediately saw the error of his ways. Since he couldn't return the money he stole from me, he signed the ranch over instead."

He uttered an incredulous laugh. "Because you pulled a gun on him?"

Her answering smile held no humor. "No, because he knew I'd shoot him."

"Shoot him?" He looked wary.

Letitia nodded. She stepped forward until her breasts brushed against his chest. "Yes, shoot him," she breathed the words. She idly fingered his belt buckle, tracing the engraved surface. She could feel Tyler take in a deep breath at her light touch. "I told Giancarlo that he should do the right thing or he would lose something he valued."

Tyler's eyes bulged. "You did?" he squeaked and coughed to clear his voice. He didn't dare move an inch. Letitia seemed to enjoy shocking him and to date, this was her best.

"I may not be fond of riding, but let me assure you I can shoot very well." She puckered up her lips in a kiss just before she turned to leave. "Good night, Tyler."

The front door closed behind her with a silent whoosh.

A burst of air exploded from Tyler's lungs as he collapsed against the porch post. "I knew that woman was lethal. I just knew it."

LETITIA HAD NO IDEA how she got back into the house and down the hall to her bedroom. She lay in bed finding it difficult to sleep. After undressing, she huddled under the covers with a book. In the end she tossed it aside because it couldn't hold her interest. Not when she was still remembering Tyler's kisses and reeling from the effect. She pushed a second pillow behind her back and stared up at the ceiling where moon shadows chased themselves across the surface.

"Maybe I should do more hard labor," she mused. "Maybe I should have a hormone test. That's it, too many hormones." With a nod of self agreement, she closed her eyes and soon fell asleep. Little did she know that Tyler was standing at the bunkhouse window, watching her bedroom light wink out and cursing her for obviously not having the problem he was.

"UH, BOSS?" One of the men, wearing a strange look on his face, approached Tyler.

Tyler looked over his shoulder. "Yeah?"

"You know how you had me go in the house to get those vaccination papers from the office?" he murmured, looking around as if afraid of being overheard.

Tyler, puzzled by the man's secretive manner, nodded. "Just spit it out, Kendall."

He leaned forward. "I don't want to say anything. Maybe you should see it for yourself. She's in the living room." He loped off.

"Where're those vaccination papers?" Tyler shouted after him. "The vet's coming out right after breakfast."

"Boss, after you see what I did, you'll understand why I clean forgot to get them," he called over his shoulder.

Tyler headed for the house without a second thought. The moment he opened the front door, a familiar man's voice reached his ears. His curiosity pushed him farther inside until he stood in the living-room doorway. He stared at the picture on the television screen without saying a word. Shaking his head, he went back to the kitchen.

"How long has this been going on?" he asked Myrna without preamble.

She cocked her head in the direction of the front of the house where faint sounds of shouting and gunshots could be heard. "Her research, you mean?"

"Her *what*?"

"Research." Myrna filled the large coffee urn she kept going all day. "She's learning about ranching."

"She's in there watching *Red River* for research?" Tyler's voice rose. "On what?"

Myrna held up a hand to shush him. "Don't you say one word to that girl," she warned, advancing on him with fire in her eyes. "She's doing it the only way she knows how."

"All she's going to learn from John Wayne is that driving cattle is hell!" He silently implored a higher being for help. None seemed forthcoming. "What's she going to watch next? *The Alamo*?"

"Her brother sent her just about every western film on tape along with an extensive selection of books on the west," she explained. "I kept her company last night and for the first time in years, had a chance to enjoy an oldie with Alan Ladd."

Tyler shook his head.

"What is she supposed to do?" Myrna demanded. "You've pretty much left her to her own devices for the past week."

He had left her alone since that night he'd kissed her and he'd learned the truth about her. He argued with himself that he had work to do and he didn't consider baby-sitting a new owner part of his duties. Although, deep down, he knew he should be showing her how to get involved.

"All right." He sighed. Surrender was much safer for one's stomach where Myrna was concerned. "I'll take care of it."

The cook faced him. "You should have done it in the beginning."

He threw up his hands. "All right! I'll take care of it first thing in the morning. Is that acceptable?" He didn't bother to blunt his sarcasm.

"I'll let you know."

"WE'RE GOING ON A TOUR of your land today," Tyler announced, spearing Letitia with a look that dared her to challenge him. Out of the corner of his eye, he could see Myrna smiling her approval of his announcement. At least his breakfast wouldn't be burned beyond recognition.

Letitia chose to ignore that telling look. "Ben's overhauling the truck's carburetor today."

"We'll be riding. The truck can't travel over some of the terrain we're heading for anyway."

"Riding?" she repeated numbly, feeling cold inside. "Horses?"

"That's the accepted mode of transportation." Tyler looked at J.T. "You can choose an appropriate mount for her," he told the older man.

"No problem."

"Riding," Letitia muttered under her breath. She looked down at her breakfast. She suddenly had no appetite.

Tyler finished his own breakfast with swift dispatch and got up. "Don't worry, countess," he whispered in her ear. "I'll make sure your royal little rear doesn't get too bruised. Hate to see valuable merchandise ruined."

"A horse is nothing more than a large dog," Letitia told herself later when she walked out to the barn. "It just neighs instead of barks."

"What's barking?" J.T. asked, hearing the last part of her self-reassurance.

"My stomach." She eyed the roan with trepidation. "Don't you have something smaller?"

"Hell, Letty, this ole boy will take you all over the land and not even breathe hard." He was clearly pleased with his choice.

Letitia rolled up the sleeves of her aqua-colored soft cotton shirt. Black jeans, boots and a black flat-brimmed hat completed her outfit. She had pulled her hair back into a french braid in deference to the warm day.

"I don't see how he has the time to do this," she grumbled, still eyeing the waiting horse. "He's supposed to be running this ranch."

"Correction, boss lady, I'm supposed to be following your orders." Tyler walked up, leading his bay stallion. "You've been here long enough to have seen your land several times over. Playtime's through, countess. Time to work." He swung into the saddle with an ease Letitia admired, and hated him for because she knew she couldn't even come close to that.

"All right, missy, up you go." J.T. offered his cupped hands for her to step into.

With J.T.'s boost, Letitia found herself seated in the broad saddle and clutching the horn. "This is a definite improvement over the English saddle," she acknowledged, taking up the reins.

"Just remember we won't be riding to the hounds today." Tyler led the way with Letitia unwillingly following.

"I'm very glad to hear that." Her teeth clacked together before she could adjust her body to her mount's rocking rhythm. "I always felt the fox got a rough deal."

Tyler didn't deliberately set a leisurely pace, but he didn't set a difficult one, either.

"Is there a reason why we're suddenly playing Boy Scouts on their annual jaunt?" she called after him, frantically trying to remember her riding instructor's words those many years ago. In the end, she only prayed she wouldn't disgrace herself and fall off.

"What is this horse's name?" she yelled, figuring Tyler wasn't going to hear her any other way. If he even bothered listening to her.

She wouldn't have felt very safe if she'd seen his wicked grin. "Son of Satan."

"He's lying," Letitia murmured, beginning to feel more comfortable in the unfamiliar saddle. "I just know he's lying. I bet his name is Barney."

As she relaxed, she felt easier about looking around to enjoy the scenery.

"At one time, more than two hundred-thousand head roamed these ranges," Tyler explained, pointing out the pasture land that seemed to go on forever. "Harvey's ancestors settled here in the eighteen-forties when there wasn't much more than the Crow roaming the land. He even had some Crow blood in him. As far as the eye could see there was cattle. Prime beef driven down to the railroad and shipped back east. They survived wars, the Depression and more wars. What they couldn't survive was the steadily dropping price of beef, then feed prices went up and running a large herd wasn't viable. Some have switched to running buffalo since the meat has gotten so popular. Surrounding ranches have looked into other ways of using the land to make a profit. You have to do something or you end up running so far in the red, it's difficult to climb out.

Letitia looked in the same direction and again noticed there weren't as many cattle as she thought there would be. She shifted her aching butt in the saddle. "What about now? Haven't things improved?"

Tyler reined in his mount. "It still isn't viable," he said baldly. "And with winters the way they are, you can't just run anything here. They have to be sturdy enough to live through deep snows and blizzards."

"So what you're saying is I have all this land, a fraction of the herd that used to be here and no money," Letitia said. She looked over the gently rolling green hills that her mind's eye could easily picture covered with cattle. "Is that pretty much it?"

"That's it exactly."

She pulled her hat down farther over her eyes to shade them from the morning sun. "Do I have any options at all?"

"You can always sell to someone who knows what they're doing. Get out before things get any worse and have some money to boot."

She shot him a I-know-what-you're-trying-to-do-and-you-won't-succeed look. "Besides that. The word is options, not option." She stressed the s sound.

Tyler leaned forward, crossing his arms on the saddle horn. "Are you serious?"

She looked him straight in the eye. "Very."

"You could try running something other than cattle."

"Sheep?" She grimaced when she saw Tyler's expression. "It *is* done, you know," she said in defense.

"Although, I guess a hard-core cattleman couldn't handle it, am I right? Well, there has to be something."

Tyler watched Letitia. He'd decided a long time ago that watching her was turning into a dangerous addiction. Today, her face was flushed from the ride and her eyes glowing. He wondered where she got all her enthusiasm to enjoy the life all around her. And if she was willing to share it with him. What really bothered him was that she was settling in too easily. The part of him that hungered for a piece of his *own* land seemed to be shrinking and he didn't like that feeling one bit. He needed her gone from his life before he took to a crazy notion about sharing this ranch.

Chapter Nine

It was time to take a break. Tyler took off his hat and wiped his arm across his forehead as he looked toward a stand of trees a short distance away.

"This looks like a good place to stop for a while and take a breather." When he reached them, he pulled on the reins and dismounted with a fluid ease Letitia alternately admired and hated. He dropped the reins, ground-tying his mount. "I can imagine you're ready for one by now."

She looked around, vainly trying to ignore the numbness that had rapidly spread up her legs and was now centered in her rear end. They'd been riding for the past two hours and after the first fifteen minutes she felt her nerve endings screaming for release from this agony. Tyler noticed her wince when she shifted in her seat.

"Sorry, it's nothing unusual for us to ride most of the day and not think anything of it." She studied him and decided he didn't look as sincerely apologetic as she'd like. Actually, she'd prefer it if he looked like he had *her* pain. "If you walk around a little, you'll get rid of any stiffness you might feel."

Letitia was convinced if she fell out of the saddle and tried to stand up, her legs would not support her. But she wasn't about to tell that to Tyler. As it was, she decided the only thing that had kept her upright in the saddle all morning was the enticing sight of Tyler as he rode in front of her pointing out various landmarks. There was nothing like a man in jeans riding a horse to fuel more than a few women's fantasies. She shifted her weight again and devoutly wished she hadn't. Her body had a way of making her miserable for doing such things. Pinpricks of sensation declared numb nerves were coming back from the dead. The last time she felt so miserable was the last time she'd ridden a horse.

"You know, everything looks so lovely from up here that I think I'll just stay in the saddle," she said brightly, shifting from side to side in hope of discovering if there was any feeling in her body at all other than agony.

His lips twitched with humor. He appeared by her leg. "Feeling a bit sore, countess?"

"You can't feel sore if you can't feel anything at all." She chose to adopt her haughty lady-of-the-manor voice. While it didn't intimidate Tyler in the least, it did make her feel better.

Tyler held up a hand. "Come on, I'll help you down."

"I can get down by myself." But she didn't argue when he grasped her waist as she tried to swing out of the saddle as easily as he did and completely failed. She held on to the saddle with an iron grip.

"Pull up some dirt," he invited, walking toward the stand of trees nearby.

"If I let go, I know I will fall very ungracefully to the ground."

Tyler chuckled at her announcement. "Sweetheart, you are something." He carefully pried her fingers from the horn and kept a firm hold on her as he walked her over to the trees. With his hands holding onto her wrists, she was able to drop down to the grass.

"Ooh," Letitia moaned as she felt the pins and needles of pain invade her lower body. "I told you I was better staying in the saddle."

"Nah, you just need more time." He sat down beside her and pulled one foot into his lap. He pulled her boot off and began massaging her toes with solid smooth strokes.

Her eyes widened as the sensation of life raced back up her leg. "That feels so good," she rasped. "Don't stop."

Tyler's head snapped upward at her words and tone of voice. "Think about saying that in another time and place," he said huskily.

Gritting her teeth against the prickling pain, Letitia leaned forward and swept the stray strands of hair from his forehead. "You know, for a country boy, you've been working awfully fast," she murmured.

His gray eyes bored into hers. "That bother you?"

"Have you heard me complaining?" Her smile seemed a bit wobbly. "Although, you may as well know now, I'm not the sexual expert you think I am. I've always been very choosy about men."

"You didn't do a very good job with Giancarlo," he pointed out.

Letitia lifted her face, allowing the morning breeze to wash over her skin. While she usually enjoyed being light and outrageous with people, she didn't feel like showing that side just now.

"The party set isn't what it used to be," she said softly as she leaned back, bracing herself on her hands. "I saw too many people fall for the wrong person and end up either jaded for life or hopelessly heartbroken. True love doesn't exist among many of them."

He studied her profile, her head thrown back and her eyes closed. "Maybe they didn't hide their true selves as well as some of the others did." There was no mistaking his meaning.

She snapped forward. "Get this straight," she gritted. "To many, my mother seemed flighty and irresponsible, but she was very strict with her children and was determined we wouldn't grow up to be shallow and immoral. I've adhered to those values, whether you think I have or not."

"Oh sure." He didn't sound sincere. She wanted to hit him. Again.

"It all comes down to Giancarlo's promise that he'd sell you the ranch and I know you're hoping I will do the same, but you have to understand how important it is that I succeed with this. I need to prove I can do something all on my own." Her face was grim with determination.

"You don't have the funds to do what's needed," he said, tight-lipped.

"And you do?" She was determined to challenge him right back.

"No, I don't," he admitted. "But I do have the knowledge. And not from watching western movies and reading books, either. Experience is what counts."

Letitia nodded, understanding where this was coming from. "You may find this hard to believe, but I did learn a few things from watching those movies." She shifted her position, brushing away a buzzing fly.

He looked skeptical. "Yeah, sure."

She was determined not to allow him to goad her. "Let me explain something. Stephano's family firmly believed the women took care of the home and had babies. They were of the old world beliefs that women did not belong in the workplace."

"And you hated it," he stated.

"At first, I was so flattered that he wanted to take care of me. He enjoyed telling people that I was his cherished possession," she explained with a small laugh. "I thought it was a joke until the day I realized he was right. I was a possession just like his stable of polo ponies and collection of Chinese erotic art." She shook her head.

"Erotic art?" Tyler drawled. "Interesting."

"That's not the point," she clipped, already seeing where his train of thought was heading. "Don't even ask about it. The point I'm making is that I was given a specific spot and I wasn't to stray from it."

He held up his hands in surrender. "Fine, so how *did* you stray from your exclusive life?"

Letitia wondered why she was even bothering. "I wanted to do more than give charity balls and dinners. I reminded Stephano that members of royalty worked actively in more than decorating the house, but that didn't matter to him. All I needed to do was give him his heir and happily spend the money he was only too happy to lavish on me." She looked pensive. "You know, a lot of women would kill to have what I had with Stephano, but to me, it wasn't enough. In the long run, I really didn't have a husband, just someone who breezed in every once in awhile with a kiss on the forehead and a piece of jewelry to make things better.''

"Yeah, it must have been real rough."

Letitia narrowed her eyes. "I should smack you silly for that crack," she gritted. "You're not even listening, are you?

"Sure, I've heard every word you said." His bland indifference sent her temper soaring even more. "Your husband treated you like a cherished little pet and made sure every luxury was at your fingertips. No wonder you got a divorce."

Letitia shook her head. She hated Tyler for his smug manner while she sat here revealing a hurtful part of her life. She controlled her temper by removing her hat and placing it in her lap, absently brushing the dust off the crown.

"I was raised to honor the vows I'd taken," she spoke in a low intense voice. "But Stephano obviously hadn't been. I soon discovered that along with his passion for polo was his passion for having affairs with his friends' wives. I'd been kept blissfully ignorant of the fact for quite some time."

Tyler immediately knew where she was headed. "Obviously, you found out when you walked in on him playing polo pony with one of his conquests."

Her head nodded in an affirmative. "I was so disgusted with what I saw, nothing he said mattered. He tried to say all the right words and make the right promises, but deep down, I knew he didn't mean them. He just didn't want me to leave until he had his son and heir. He even tried to offer me a huge settlement if I promised to stay until we had a child," she concluded bitterly. "I told him he may have been Italian and the courts frowned on divorce, but if he didn't give me my freedom, I would do all I could to make his life a living hell any way I could. He knew I not only meant it, but that I could do it. He didn't fight me. I packed up Le Chat and moved to Salem to be with Jack after that."

There were so many sides to her, he wondered if he'd ever see all of them. "From an Italian palace to haunted bedroom with a lecherous old ghost who liked to watch you undress." He slowly scanned her body from head to toe, pausing at the creamy swells barely visible in the open neck of her shirt.

"Old Humphrey was harmless. The man may have been dead, but he didn't consider himself out of the game. Maybe I gave him some joy. I doubt he'd had much in the last hundred years."

Tyler shook his head. He touched a stray curl that had escaped her braid, winding it around his finger until it rested against her cheek. Her skin was warm and silky, silently inviting him closer. He wondered if she knew just how tempted he was to do all the things he'd been dreaming about. He leaned over farther.

"You like to tempt fate, don't you? To see how far you can push someone before they fall into a pit of insanity," he murmured.

She slowly turned her head. A fraction more on her part and their lips would touch. She could smell the rich aroma of soap coupled with sweaty male and horse. She considered it more arousing than any man's cologne on the market.

"I don't seem to be succeeding with you," she whispered, not caring that her hat was slipping off her lap.

He wanted to throw his head back and laugh until he was sore. Then he wanted to strip off her clothes and make love to her until he was sore. "Lady, you've succeeded with me more than you'll ever know."

"And you hate it, don't you?" Letitia ran her fingertips down his cheek, feeling the rough skin rasp the sensitive pads. Years of exposure to the harsh elements had deepened the lines and added a rugged texture to his face. His gray eyes were dark with desire and seemed to burn their way to her very soul. She looked down and picked up one of his hands, pulling the leather glove off. She traced the lines in his palm, studied the callused tips and a nasty-looking cut along the back of his hand.

"You always seem to have a bruise or a cut somewhere," she murmured.

"Hazards of the job." He felt the effects of her touch all the way down his gut. He never knew he could feel so aroused just by a woman touching his hand, but he discovered Letitia had a special way with her soft hands and feather-light touches. He shifted his weight as his jeans started to strangle him. He felt his breath slam out of his chest when she smiled. "You like to tempt men, don't you? You like to be seen like something from a dream."

"I thought I was more like something out of a nightmare."

"If you were, I need to look into having nightmares more often." It took all his self-control not to take her in his arms. "I'm still trying to figure you out, Letitia Jones DeMarco."

"Is that why you spend so much time peering in my bedroom window?" Her smile widened when she saw his surprise. "You really should put some curtains up there, Mr. Barnes. I thought you'd stopped smoking. J.T. once mentioned the bet you and he had going."

He stiffened. "Spying, countess?"

"Who's spying? I was just taking in some night air. A lit cigarette is as good as a nightlight to point someone out." Letitia pushed her rear end forward until she could comfortably lay down on the grass. "And I had curtains to shield me."

Tyler stretched out beside her, bracing his head on his fist. "So you're admitting you were spying, too."

"Only when I saw the lit cigarette."

"How did you know it was me?" he demanded. "It could have been any one of the men hoping to catch you with your clothes off."

"Another man would have given up when he realized he wasn't going to catch me naked," she softly countered. "That's when I knew I wasn't dealing with a pervert. Just you," she added deliberately.

A corner of his mouth moved upward. He played with the top button of her shirt until it came loose.

A spot of sunlight bounced off his chin, she idly noticed, magnifying a faint growth of dark beard.

"Does this bother you?"

"Should it?" Letitia countered. "I guess it goes along with the foreplay we've been engaging in for the past few weeks. And that isn't even close to the real thing."

Tyler's dry chuckle skipped along her nerve endings. "Sweetheart, I don't think you have anything to worry about. If we ever come up against the real thing it will turn out to be so good between us you won't want to stop." His fingers edged their way inside her shirt.

She batted his hand away. "Keep your hands to yourself, cowboy."

"That's not what you said the last time." He loosened a few more buttons and parted the material with his fingertip. A sharp breath escaped when he exposed a lace-edged bra that barely covered the creamy mounds of flesh.

"Don't believe in plain white cotton, do you?" he asked in a hoarse voice as he fingered the dark taupe lace edging pale mocha silk.

"I didn't think you'd find it as interesting," she whispered with a sardonic twist.

"Interesting isn't the word for it. It's a good thing I didn't know about this before we started out or we wouldn't have made it any farther than the barn." His brows met together in a curious frown before he found the tiny clip fastener between her breasts. He looked up, checking her expression before he flicked it loose.

Letitia rapidly sat up and pulled her blouse together. "Enough."

"Not yet." He boldly splayed his palm against her bare abdomen before she could finish rebuttoning her shirt. "Live dangerously, countess. That does seem to be what you do best."

She turned her head. "Good idea," she whispered, pulling his mouth down to hers. "I like a man who thinks he can take me on and live to tell the . . ." The last word was smothered by his mouth.

Letitia was convinced fireworks exploded overhead as Tyler's warmth covered her. She purred with delight when his hand slipped inside the gaping shirt to cover one breast, his thumb gently flicking her nipple. She wanted to scream when his mouth replaced his hand.

"So sweet," he murmured, curling his tongue around her nipple.

"Tyler." In her agitation to feel more of his bare skin, she ripped open his shirt, sending buttons flying everywhere. She ran her hands along his chest, feeling his muscles tense under her caressing palms. She lifted her head and tongued a copper-colored nipple until it hardened into a tiny nub. She laughed softly at his murmured curse when she moved her hands downward. "My, my, is this why they call Montana the Big Sky Country?"

His reply was to kiss her so thoroughly she could only hang on to him. Before she could take a breath to calm her jangling senses, he rotated his palm against the juncture between her thighs. She gasped and arched upward under his touch.

"Slow and gentle, baby," he whispered. "Slow and gentle."

"That's easy for you to say." She struggled for air.

"Call it getting even for your little trick with the carrot that day." He nibbled her ear lobe.

"I understand it's your favorite vegetable." She was positive neon colors were flashing before her eyes.

He chuckled. "Well, that little stunt you pulled in the kitchen gave it a whole new meaning." He moved until he lay securely between her parted thighs. He muttered explicit words of praise as he greedily kissed and nipped every inch of bare flesh her open shirt revealed. "I want you, Letitia." His breath was warm against her stomach. He fingered the metal button and zipper tab as he looked at her with a molten silver gaze.

Her breath caught in her throat. Tyler didn't need to say the words to her. She only had to feel his arousal bulging against her thigh. "Not here," she panted, struggling to sit up.

Tyler gently pushed her back and crept upward kissing her deeply again until any thoughts of leaving vanished from her brain.

"All right. Uncle," she gasped, pulling away. "If we keep this up much longer, I'm going to seriously think about ripping off all of your clothing and having my wicked way with you." She scooted backward on her rump until she could sit up. Tyler sat cross-legged across from her looking wonderfully sexy with his shirt open and hanging outside his jeans and hair mussed. She frowned. "Where's your hat?"

He grinned. "You threw it like a Frisbee right after you ripped my shirt open."

She clapped hands over burning cheeks as she realized his shirt was missing most of its buttons. "I can't believe I did that. I've never done anything like that before."

"You said you like to live dangerously, so I figured ripping open men's shirts was second nature to you."

"I probably thought I was ripping out your heart."

Tyler trapped her hands between his before she could inflict injury. "Last I looked, my heart wasn't that far down on my body."

Letitia snatched her hands back and turned to pick up her hat. Fiddling with the strings helped her mentally find her balance. She smoothed flyaway strands of hair from her face and took several deep cleansing breaths to calm herself.

Looking unruffled and as if the last few minutes hadn't happened, Tyler stood up. Staring at his open shirt, he arched an eyebrow at Letitia as if to say it's your doing, shrugged and leisurely tucked his shirt into his jeans. He leaned down to grab her hand and pull her to her feet.

"I better get you back to the house before Myrna sends out a search party," he told her.

She arched a disbelieving eyebrow as she quickly fastened each of her shirt buttons under Tyler's enigmatic gaze.

"Feel better that you've called a halt?" he asked.

"Immensely." She picked her hat up and slapped it against her hip. "I guess my idea of true western romance is—" she tapped her forefinger against her chin in exaggerated thought "—you playing your guitar and serenading me under my window."

"Good thing I don't have a guitar since it's not my style."

"You could borrow one." Letitia picked up the reins and tried to pull herself up into the saddle without much success.

Tyler boosted her up. "There's only two drawbacks to your idea, countess," he drawled.

"No, it can't be!" She clapped her hands to her cheeks in mock astonishment. "Don't tell me that you can't play a guitar. A cowboy who can't play a guitar? I would think an atrocity like that could get you thrown out of the union."

He grinned. "Not only that. I can't sing. I'm about as tone deaf as you can get. I'm not even allowed to sing in the shower."

Letitia looked down her nose at him.

"Well, then what use are you if you can't play a guitar or sing?" she playfully demanded.

His hand on her thigh sent shivers of delight down her spine. "Don't worry, I'll be only too happy to show you when the time comes, and you won't have anything to complain about.''

"Only if you think you can outwit me into selling you the ranch.''

His eyes turned dark silver shaded with purpose. "I wouldn't have to outwit you if you realized I deserve it fair and square.''

"Fair and square?'' Letitia asked archly. "This is *my* ranch Tyler, and though I may need the time, there's no doubt I'll soon know enough to competently run it.''

Tyler kept a firm grip on her thigh. His fingers had a habit of stroking oh, so lightly in a way that sent quivers along her nerve endings.

"When pigs fly.'' He carefully enunciated each word.

She leaned over and gave his cheek a condescending pat. "Guess what, Mr. Barnes,'' she whispered, deliberately puckering her lips with each word. Anyone seeing them from a distance would think she was blowing him loving kisses. "I just saw Porky Pig in his SuperPig costume soar overhead.'' She straightened up in the saddle and gathered the reins. "And you know what that means.''

"Yeah, that you need your eyesight checked.''

She laughed. "Don't be a sore loser, Tyler. It doesn't become you.''

That was when Tyler became determined to guide Letitia over the roughest terrain he could find on the way back.

"Let's see just how tough she really is,'' he murmured, feeling better already.

Chapter Ten

"May he fall into a bog somewhere and rot there," Letitia muttered under her breath as she slowly slid her way out of the saddle. Tyler hadn't offered to help her down and she'd be damned before she'd ask. The minute her feet hit solid ground she could feel the aches and pains shoot through her thighs.

"Are you doing all right over there?" Tyler asked with mock solicitude. "No problems?"

"Just dandy!" She brightened her voice long enough to answer, then darkly muttered, "I'm going to set Le Chat on him right after I sharpen his little claws."

"I assume you know how to take care of your mount?" Tyler asked, walking toward her.

"Naturally." After making sure her mount was properly cooled off, under Tyler's amused gaze as he watched her stiff posture, Letitia led Son of Satan into the barn and began wiping the horse down. Her little imp of mischief whispered in her ear as she noticed Tyler still watching her.

"There's something very soothing about a massage, isn't there, Satan, old boy?" she crooned to the horse as she ran the sponge down his flanks. "You realize it's all in the hands, don't you? Hands that need to be gentle yet strong as they find all your favorite little spots." She kept a corner of her eye on Tyler who'd immediately straightened up as he heard her words. "Personally, I prefer using a nice rich cream or silky lotion for my massages, but I don't think you'd appreciate that as much as I do. There's nothing like the cool lotion gliding over your bare skin, warming in the process." By now, she noticed a faint sheen of perspiration on Tyler's forehead. He looked as if his boots had been nailed to the floor and he couldn't have moved from that spot if he wanted to.

Letitia bent from the waist, taking her time looking for a cloth while giving Tyler a good view of her rear end slowly swaying from side to side. The movement sent frantic signals from her body to her brain that what she was doing was painful, but she didn't care. She'd do whatever was necessary to make Tyler feel like a sex-starved maniac.

"Too bad we can't have candlelight in here, Satan," she continued cooing to the horse as she later finished by gently combing his mane and tail. "Maybe even some incense to add to the atmosphere." Her soft words grew even softer as she completed her task and carried the equipment out of the stall. "Well, I'm finished." She made sure her voice was loud and strong to break the spell. Tyler jerked upright as if rudely awakened from a lovely dream.

"Good," he said tersely.

As Letitia carefully made her way back to the house, she noticed Tyler wasn't far behind. She gritted her teeth and forced her aching legs to walk as naturally as possible.

Myrna looked up at they entered the kitchen. Her eyes widened at the sight of Letitia's slightly stiff movements and bright red face. As her gaze fell on the man behind her, she did a double take when she realized that even though Tyler's shirt was tucked into his jeans, it gaped open. She could only assume it had to do with the absence of buttons. She bit down hard on her lower lip to keep from laughing. She would have paid a small fortune to know what happened during their ride! Although, now they looked as if a major war was soon to be reenacted.

"Gracious, Tyler, what did you do to the poor girl? Force her to ride into the sun all morning?" She shook her head at her first sight of Letitia's sunburned face. "Couldn't you see what sensitive skin she has?" She opened the refrigerator and pulled out a small jar. "Aloe gel," she explained, handing it to Letitia. "You better smooth it over your face so you don't peel."

Tyler's features displayed concern as he realized just how painfully red Letitia's face was. "I should have made sure your hat was pulled down far enough to shade your face."

She shrugged. "I'll be fine," she assured him, temporarily forgetting her vow to show Tyler she knew what she was doing. She had no idea Myrna was watching them.

Apparently liking what she saw, the cook nodded and returned to her tasks.

"You better drink this up," Tyler told her as he poured orange juice into two glasses and handed one to Letitia.

She drank deeply of the cold liquid and immediately filled the glass again.

"Mr. Beecham called," Myrna announced. "He'd like you to stop by this afternoon at one."

Letitia grimaced. "I should have called him sooner. I wanted to be the one to make the overture."

"Better you than me," Myrna mumbled, peeling potatoes with sudden industry.

Letitia looked from one to the other. "Meaning?"

Tyler was the one to reply. "Let's just say old banker Beecham isn't one of the most popular people in the county."

"What banker is? What's his problem? Hard-nosed? Drinks in secret or does he like the ladies?" she teased.

"Hard-nosed?" Myrna snorted. "Listen to this. His son-in-law needed to apply for a short-term loan to pay his wife's hospital expenses after their baby was born. The baby was two weeks premature and needed additional care. Micah insisted on collateral before he'd even consider looking at the application! His excuse was he needed to make sure the boy would pay back his loan. That just because he was family didn't mean he should expect special consideration."

Letitia felt her morning jubilation ebb. "Well, maybe the son-in-law wasn't reliable to begin with," she said weakly.

Tyler shook his head. "Adam is one of the most honest and industrious people you can meet. It was because he doesn't wear a white shirt and tie to work that bothers old man Beecham. He's a mechanic," he explained.

Letitia sighed, visualizing a pleasant meeting going down the tubes. "Then it's a good thing I've had experience with rigid thinking, old-fashioned people like him," she explained, sounding more positive than she felt as she headed for the phone. "I'll just act like a sweet little lady and everything will be fine."

Tyler shook his head. "Do you want to tell her more about him or shall I?" he asked Myrna.

"Let her find out on her own," she advised, walking out of the kitchen. "She's eager to meet with everyone on their terms. She might as well find out it can't always work out her way." She stared pointedly at his open shirt.

"I guess I better get back out," Tyler edged his way toward the back door. He wanted to escape before Myrna cornered him with some personal questions. The woman was worse than his mother had ever been!

"Tyler?" Her voice stopped him dead in his tracks.

"Yeah."

"I'd hide that shirt if I were you. The men might wonder just as much as I do how you lost all the buttons."

He cursed under his breath as he slipped out the door. "Good idea."

LETITIA BUSIED HERSELF gathering up all the paperwork she'd need for the meeting. She only hoped she could put off suffering any more aches and pains until she got back to the ranch. A long hot shower hadn't helped much except show her just how bruised and battered she felt.

"My whole life has turned around," she murmured, pushing the papers into a manila folder. "Up at dawn, eating probably three times my body weight, having a cowboy drive me crazy." The last lingered on her tongue like the aftereffects of a fine wine and left a smile on her lips. She didn't notice the smile stayed there as she dressed and applied her makeup.

TYLER DECIDED HE WAS going to drive Letitia to the bank whether she wanted him to or not. He took some time to wash up after he cleaned out the truck.

"What is she planning to do?" J.T. asked, holding a trash bag open as Tyler swept out empty pop cans and cigarette wrappers. Tyler gazed at the mess, realizing the last time the truck had been cleaned out was the day he'd picked up Letitia at the airport.

"She thinks she can charm old man Beecham into extending the loan," Tyler gritted.

The older man chuckled. "That's 'cause she hasn't met him yet. Not even a pretty face like hers will get him to part with money easy. You'd think he owned all of it the way he's so tight with loans."

"We had to have the vet out four times last month for emergencies. Operating expenses increased and income decreased," he said grimly. "She may not know ranching, but she can read the figures I give her. If something isn't done pretty soon, she could lose the ranch and she knows it."

"Her brother's rich. She could ask him for a loan to tide her over."

"If you were her, would you?"

J.T. sighed, recognizing Tyler's meaning. "Then we all better pray she can charm that old boy."

Tyler's senses went on alert as something in the air warned him of a tornado on the way. A tornado named Letitia. He straightened up and turned around to find her walking down the steps.

"Holy cow," he breathed, unable to take his eyes off the vision walking toward him.

J.T. stared at Letitia with frank awe. "Well, if anyone can get Beecham to part with bucks, it should be her."

Letitia smiled at them. "Gentlemen," she greeted them. "I thought I'd try for the professional, yet feminine, look. Think I'll pass?" She turned around slowly with her arms held out.

"I know I'd sure open the vault if you smiled that pretty at me," J.T. announced, before leaving them alone.

Letitia looked expectantly at Tyler, but he didn't seem to have anything to say. He was too busy admiring her slender form garbed in a black silk suit that set off her honey blond coloring. Black hosiery and pumps completed the outfit with only a hint of aqua lace that matched her eyes exactly, peeking out of the deep V-neckline of the suit jacket. She'd pinned her hair low on the back of her neck in an intricate coil. She looked professional and beautiful. Tyler just didn't have the heart to tell her she looked too professional and too big city for a small-town banker. Beecham was convinced he was the county's answer to sophistication since he vacationed in New York City every year.

"You'll make him sit up and take notice," he said abruptly, assisting her into the passenger seat. He couldn't help but notice how her skirt hiked up to reveal an extensive length of thigh and a black lace garter fastening a sheer black stocking. He swallowed the stone threatening to take root in his throat. He had a feeling it was going to be a long drive.

"I wish I could speak with a southern accent," Letitia fretted, as they barreled down the highway.

That was a new one in his book. "Why a southern accent?"

"Because men turn to putty when they hear a woman speak with a southern accent. One of the girls at college was from Savannah. Her father was with the American embassy. All she had to do was bat those baby blues and lay on a sugary drawl and she had the professors eating out of her hand," she explained. "I don't know what it is. The best I can do is a passable Italian accent, but it doesn't work the same as a good drawl."

"If Mrs. Higgins can survive Beecham, you can," Tyler said casually. Too casually.

She eyed him suspiciously. "Who's Mrs. Higgins?"

He shrugged. "I don't think you need to worry about it."

Letitia held out her hand, idly inspecting her nails. "Maybe not, but why not let me in on the story?" Her sweet voice was laced with strychnine.

He shrugged as if it was no matter to him. "Mrs. Higgins has been a widow for the last thirty years who's always done things her way. Including writing out her checks but not signing them. She always feared someone would learn to copy her signature and forge checks on her account. Since she'd dealt with the bank for more than fifty years, no one thought anything about it. Until Mr. Beecham informed her she either began signing her checks or the bank would start refusing them. Well, she ignored him and her checks started bouncing all over the place because old man Beecham ordered them sent back."

"I can imagine she wasn't too happy about that," she mused, already visualizing a modern-day Scrooge. "I know I wouldn't be. He should have taken steps to explain to her they could watch out for her, not give threats."

"There's more," he went on, catching a glance of her in the corner of his eye. She did look a bit unsettled. Good.

"More?" She was surprised. "What more could he do than refuse to honor the checks? Although, I would think the people she wrote them out to would complain about this man."

"Beecham is a law unto himself," Tyler said bluntly. "Mrs. Higgins decided to be the one to take action. She waited until Mr. Beecham left the bank at lunchtime and she told him loud and clear how she thought he was the meanest man in town and he deserved everything he got. When he basically told her to get lost, she began hitting him over the head with her umbrella." There was no missing her wide eyes and stunned expression.

"She hit him with her umbrella?" She giggled. "I love it! This is one woman I'd dearly like to meet."

Tyler shook his head. "She still got a raw deal, Letitia. He closed her account and Mrs. Higgins was out a very good umbrella."

Letitia kept her feelings of unease to herself. "I'll make sure to find a very strong umbrella," she asserted, settling back in the seat. Her posture indicated she would prefer silence. Tyler was only too happy to comply.

She looked around as Tyler cruised the business section of the town. Clothing shops for all ages, a Sears catalog store on one corner and gas station on the other, hardware and a video store. She studied the people sauntering down the sidewalk. She started to exclaim to Tyler when she saw a man who was clearly a full-blooded Native American, then subsided. If she was going to settle in here, she had to learn to act like a long-time resident.

"The town seems busy," she commented instead.

"They get a lot of steady business from the surrounding ranches and tourists stopping by a craft co-op run by the Crow," he replied.

"Something for everyone," she reflected.

She smiled when they drove past the town square with its benches and gray-haired men sitting there probably reminiscing about the past, she decided. Tyler had parked the truck in front of the bank. He climbed out and walked around to help her down. She reached back for her envelope of paperwork. She marched up to the sidewalk with her head held high, shoulders back, her manner one of a woman who knew exactly where she was going. Tyler immediately thought of Daniel entering the lions' den.

As Letitia entered the old-fashioned bank building, she idly noticed the year 1875 etched into the cornerstone.

"One of Beecham's ancestors built it," Tyler explained when she commented on the date. "I guess you could say banking's in their blood. They sure couldn't ranch worth a damn."

The moment Letitia walked into the shadowy interior, she felt as if she was under inspection and somehow had been found wanting.

"Good afternoon." She smiled warmly at the receptionist who couldn't have been less than seventy. In fact, she noticed almost all the employees were above forty. Obviously they preferred more seasoned personnel, she silently reflected and applauded. "I'm Mrs. DeMarco. I have an appointment with Mr. Beecham."

The woman nodded as she took in every stitch of Letitia's clothing and seemed to find something wanting. "He'll be with you in a moment." She looked past Letitia toward Tyler. "Tyler, haven't seen you around here in quite awhile," she commented in her dry tone.

"I've been pretty busy, Ida," he replied. "You're looking well."

"Only 'cause I take my iron tonic every morning," she pronounced, fixing him with a steely look. "You should think about taking something for yourself. You're not getting any younger. If you don't take care of your body now, it won't take care of you later on."

"I'll keep that in mind," he said a little too jovially although his tanned features looked a bit gray around the edges. He shifted his weight from one foot to the other, looking like a little boy listening to a lecture from his teacher.

Ida's head snapped up and down in agreement. "You do that. Your health isn't something you should ignore."

Letitia bit her lower lip to keep her smile hidden. She decided watching a chastened Tyler receive this lecture was vastly entertaining.

"Mrs. DeMarco."

Letitia looked up to see a tall, cadaverous man standing in an open office doorway. He wore a brown suit that had been-out-of-date for possibly the last thirty years. She was positive she was looking at the man who stood guard at the gates of hell.

"Yes," she whispered.

"Here." Tyler pushed the folder into her limp hands.

She gazed frantically at him. "You're not coming in?"

"Not my place. After all, you keep reminding me you're the boss." He gave her a little push. "Don't worry, you'll do fine. Remember, he's going to treat you like a long lost daughter."

She forced her feet to move her forward. "I don't think I want to be a member of his family."

"Well, Mrs. DeMarco, we finally meet." Micah Beecham showed her to a chair alongside his large old-fashioned rolltop desk. Try as she might, Letitia couldn't find anything to suggest modern times in the office. The chair she sat in wasn't meant for the comfort of his visitors. Walnut bookcases held dusty tomes dealing with the financial history of the state, the only source of light besides the overhead lamp was a large window, and Mr. Beecham's desk didn't hold a calculator nor a computer terminal. She wasn't surprised when he pulled out a fountain pen as he perused the papers in front of him then looked up to face her with piercing dark eyes that she swore belonged on a vulture.

"I understand when the deed to Running Springs Ranch was signed over to you, you also took over all debts pertaining to the ranch," he said in his dry wheezy voice.

"That's correct." She resisted the urge to cross her legs at the knee. A little leg wouldn't accomplish anything with this man. Instead, she opted for the ladylike crossed ankles. "I hope you realize that I've only been in Montana for a few weeks and am still learning the operation. That's why I hadn't contacted you before. I wanted to have all the facts before we talked."

He shook his head. "It wouldn't have mattered. It's been losing money for years, Mrs. DeMarco. I'd advise you sell out before we are forced to repossess the property."

She licked her suddenly dry lips. "I read the papers and the next payment isn't due for another three months."

She could swear there was no emotion on his angular face. "Except the last payment hadn't been made. The loan is in default. The only reason I haven't processed the paperwork sooner is because you are new and I knew you'd be in soon to take care of it."

"With penalty charges, how much does that come to?"

Letitia saw spots before her eyes as the man handed her a sheet of paper with the figures written on it.

"I would need some time," she said softly. *Say ten or twelve years.*

He considered her request. "I could be generous and give you five days."

Letitia mustered up her winning smile. "Mr. Beecham, you have to understand that my funds are tied up in Italy. I'm in the process of having them released and transferred over, but it does take time," she lied without batting an eyelash.

"The way I heard it, your ex-husband died and his family cut off your income."

Her smile briefly dimmed. She leaned forward to give him a whiff of her perfume. She'd made sure there wasn't any deep cleavage to admire. That was never her style. "A minor technicality. Now, I'm sure if we put our heads together we can come up with a reasonable plan. Can't we?" She settled back in her chair and waited for his reply. She was confident he could only agree with her. After all, she wasn't being unreasonable. She just needed time to figure out what she could do. If nothing else, she had confidence she could come up with something.

TYLER PRACTICALLY MANGLED his hat's brim as he sat in a hard-backed chair pinned like a helpless insect under Ida's steely gaze as she talked about the latest tonics and herbal cures. He'd forgotten how fanatic the woman was about curing the body's internal workings with seaweed or other noxious concoctions. He just wished Letitia would hurry up before Ida brought out something she thought might pep him up.

It was a good thing that Letitia couldn't care less about the latest vitamin regimen. Come to think of it, Letitia was as much a law unto herself as Ida was. She gave as good as she got and didn't believe in backing down from a battle. He enjoyed her company and all its drawbacks more than he'd enjoyed a woman in a long time. The idea was downright scary! He could feel his back breaking into a sweat as the situation started to fall into place. Lord, he couldn't be falling for her, could he?

"Talk about punishment," he muttered, shaking his head in disbelief.

"Thank you for your time, Mr. Beecham."

Her soft voice brought him out of his musings. His head snapped up as she was ushered out of the office by the grim-looking man.

"I will see you next week, Mrs. DeMarco." Mr. Beecham made it a statement.

She smiled as her proffered hand was held in his dry grasp. "Of course." When she turned toward Tyler, he noticed her smile hadn't reached her eyes.

"I guess he didn't recognize you as a relative," Tyler commented after they left the bank.

"The man shouldn't be a banker. He's a natural undertaker," she snapped. "Then he'd have a legitimate reason to take your blood, too."

"No refinancing? No extension?"

She shook her head as she tried to make her brain work at double speed. "That arrogant ass! I wish I'd had my gun with me. Then we'd see who was in charge!"

He jammed his hands in his pockets and rocked back on his heels. "Tried to tell you."

She rounded on him, fully prepared to do murder. "Oh, shut up before I use that gun on you!"

He followed at a safe distance. "Hey, I'm not the one who lost the battle."

"I did not lose anything," she spat. "I have an extension of sorts. Five days to make up past payments that Giancarlo missed." Her lips tightened. "I knew I should have shot him that day."

"Want to stop for a drink before heading back?"

"Don't tempt me." She looked up with a speculative gaze. "You men are all alike. You think you know more than women."

"We do."

"I suggest you stop right there if you don't want to walk back to the ranch," she warned, pulling open the truck door with more force than necessary. She climbed in, affording Tyler another provocative view of a black silk-stockinged leg with a hint of black lace garter.

He gulped and looked around to make sure no one else noticed the sexy sight.

It took all of Tyler's willpower not to spin her around and kiss her right then and there on the street.

He coughed to clear his throat. "Yeah, we'll get right back."

"Might as well since I have to be back again in five days." Letitia went on to sputter dire predictions of Mr. Beecham's death.

"Then let's see how fast we can make this baby go."

Once in the truck, Letitia slipped off her pumps and sighed with relief as she wiggled her toes.

"I can't believe I once considered high heels a necessary part of my wardrobe," she groaned.

"Well, they do something very nice for your legs," he observed, swinging in behind the steering wheel and starting up the truck.

Letitia pulled the pins out of her hair and combed her fingers through it. She massaged her aching scalp with the pads of her fingers as she frantically tried to come up with a solution to her problem. She refused to call Jack for help.

"When I said I wanted a chance to prove I could do something on my own, I thought I could start out with something small," she muttered, talking more to herself than to her interested audience. "Such as deciding what color to paint the house or whether the truck needed a new part. Or wondering if we need to add more cows to the herd or however you do it. I didn't expect this." She closed her eyes, but all she saw was brightly colored numbers in the amount she owed. She unbuttoned her suit jacket to reveal the aqua laced camisole that was opaque enough to double as a blouse.

Tyler's hand jerked on the gearshift as he saw the bare skin and scrap of silk. There was no question that she wasn't wearing a bra. The curved neckline caressed the top swells of her breasts.

"Maybe you should have opened the jacket while you talked to him," he said wryly under his breath.

She continued massaging her temples. "Did you say something?"

"Nope, not a thing." He changed gears with a frantic jerk of the hand.

Letitia turned to stare out the window. A sign up ahead caught her attention.

"Willow Bend sounds more like a town."

Tyler made a face as they passed the road with an ornate copper archway welcoming one and all to the Willow Bend Ranch. "More like a tourist trap. Willow Bend is a rapidly growing dude ranch."

She strained to see past the fence but could only see a scattering of buildings in the distance. One large corral filled with children riding horses in a circle was easier to see. "Big?"

"Too big."

"And they're making money?"

"Rolling in it." He was disgusted with the entire conversation.

She was amused by his revulsion. "And you don't like rolling in money?"

"Oh, I like rolling in money as good as the next person. But then I guess you already know the feeling," he dangled the bait.

She refused to bite. "How do the guests arrive?"

"There's a van that picks them up at the airport in Butte. They even have a helicopter pad at the ranch for those with the money to afford a private helicopter service." His mouth twisted with distaste. "There's plenty of friendly ranch hands to teach riding and roping, barbecues every night, a heated pool and spa, even a barber and beauty salon on the premises so the ladies don't have to worry about all that nasty dirt doing funny things to their hair. They even hold those cattle drives like in the movie so the paying guests feel like they're getting a taste of the real west." His sarcastic drawl indicated something altogether different.

"I feel sorry for the cattle," Letitia commented, idly chewing on a nail. The moment she realized what was going on, she stopped. "Someone like me herding cattle could be a frightening thought for any self-respecting cow. No, I couldn't do it. While I need money as much as the next person, I don't need it badly enough to turn the ranch into a western bed and breakfast. That wouldn't be right."

Tyler looked over at her, vainly trying to keep his eyes off her legs, which were crossed at the knee, and one foot swinging up and down in slow motion. "Keep it up, countess, and you just might win my respect."

Letitia smiled. That he might be in the beginning throes of changing his mind about her was an instant pick-me-up.

She leaned forward, allowing him a nice view of creamy bare skin against the aqua silk and cooed in his ear as she ran her fingernail down his cheek. "Oh, cowboy, by now you should know that I always win. And I firmly believe in the saying, Winner Take All."

Chapter Eleven

Tyler stood under a cold shower for fifteen minutes but knew that even if he was buried in ice cubes it wouldn't help his problem. He still didn't know how he managed to make it back to the ranch in one piece after Letitia's provocative statement about winning. He closed his eyes and lifted his face to the fast stream of water.

It would have been so easy to pull over to the side of the road and see just who would end up the winner. He considered it a major miracle that he arrived at the ranch sane.

When they pulled up near the barn, the hands were just going in for supper. Tyler grimly watched Letitia button her jacket back up. He would have preferred if it could have been buttoned all the way to her neck. The men glanced at Letitia, took a second look and then moved off when Tyler sent them silent messages that threatened murder if they didn't back off.

After his shower, he dressed and wondered if there was a way he could casually leave the bunkhouse without anyone noticing when he left and when he got back. He also knew it was next to impossible. While his room was separate from the other men, it didn't have a door he could sneak out of.

"No, you don't do it that way, you idiot! First you punch this button *then* this one. Didn't you listen to the man when he explained it to us? Here, let me do it. 'Wheel of Fortune' comes on in ten minutes and I don't intend to miss my first chance of seeing Vanna White in color," J.T. growled, snatching an elaborate remote control unit out of one of the men's hands and punching in the appropriate commands.

"'Wheel of Fortune?'" One of the men snorted, looking up from the large multicolored guide. "It says here that 'Roller Derby Mamas' is coming on. Aren't we going to see that?"

"I want to watch that Chinese Ping-Pong tournament and find out why they consider it such a hot sport," another argued. "'Sides, it's cultural."

Tyler watched the commotion with mild amusement as the men argued over the programming. Then grew impatient. "If you children can't behave there won't be any television tonight." He raised his voice to be heard above the din.

"C'mon, Tyler, this is something new for us," Ben pleaded, but still keeping his eyes riveted on the screen. "It was really nice of her brother to send a satellite dish and TV for us, too."

Tyler didn't agree. "Nice, hell. He must be nuts to do this," he muttered, walking outside after declining to join in a poker game with those who he considered had good sense. The minute he stepped outside and saw the lights shining in the main house, he knew what he had to do. The lady was going to listen to what he had to say whether she liked it or not!

Letitia appeared at the front door before he had a chance to knock.

"Come on in." She grabbed his hand and pulled him inside. "Myrna decided to stay and watch Schwarzenegger's latest film. If I have to look at those overgrown muscles another minute I'm going to scream."

"I've always been a Michelle Pfeiffer fan, myself," he said dryly. "Can we go to your office?"

"I was just going there myself." She led him down the hallway. Why don't you sit down while I get us something to drink." She disappeared before he had a chance to say a word.

Tyler looked around, impressed with the change in the once cluttered office. Letitia had most definitely put her stamp on the room.

The desk surface was cleared and polished to a high shine, the file cabinets didn't look as stuffed and the books were neatly put away. A brightly colored crocheted throw improved the looks of the couch and a portable CD player on a file cabinet played soft music. He remembered how much he hated the musty smell of Harvey's cheap cigars. The odor kept him from entering the office any more than he needed to. Now all he found was the enticing scent of Letitia's perfume. The problem was that now, he would have preferred Harvey's godawful cigars.

"Here we are," Letitia announced cheerfully as she balanced a filled plate and two glasses of wine. "Here, make yourself useful." She handed him the glasses.

Tyler looked dubiously at the wine. "Myrna usually keeps some beer in the fridge."

"Wine goes much better with snickerdoodles." She plopped down on the couch beside him. "Actually, milk probably does, but I've never been fond of it. Wine, I can handle.''

He eyed the cinnamon sugar-topped cookies with curiosity. ''Don't you believe in chocolate chip or oatmeal raisin?''

''Try it.'' She picked up a cookie and gently pushed it into his mouth. ''They're almost as good as sex,'' she crooned.

Tyler coughed so hard he almost blew a bite of cookie across the room.

Letitia immediately took one of the wine glasses and urged him to take a sip. ''Are you all right?'' She patted his back.

''You are something else,'' he wheezed, pushing the wine glass back at her. ''What are you trying to do? Kill me?''

''I said they were *almost* as good as sex, not *as* good as,'' she said wide-eyed. Except the laughter lurking in her eyes betrayed her.

It took a good deal of self-control to hang on to his reason for being there. ''I didn't come here for cookies and wine,'' he growled, putting the glasses aside and setting the plate on the floor.

Letitia smiled as she uncoiled her legs from under her and stretched them out along the couch, playfully nudging his thigh with her toes. ''I didn't think you had. I was just trying to be the polite hostess. Dare I hope you came to see me?''

''Oh, I came over here to see you, but not the way you probably think.'' He stood up and walked across the room, keeping his back to her while he sorted out his thoughts. He wished he'd thought more about this before storming in. Especially after he got a good look at her coral lacy leggings and matching crocheted short-sleeved top that covered a matching silk tank top. He grimly reminded himself that the ranch women he knew didn't dress like that. Sure, women's fashions weren't pure western out here, but they still weren't anything like the little outfits Letitia wore.

"So-o-o," she drew the word out. "Why are you here?"

Tyler spun around. "Why in the hell did you have your brother give the men a TV and satellite dish?" he roared.

Letitia reared back at the unexpected blast. "Excuse me?"

"Do you know what the men are doing over there right now?" he demanded, pointing in the direction of the bunkhouse.

"Doing whatever you men do every night," she replied, confused by his verbal rampage. "And as I feel we're talking about a guy thing here, I really wouldn't want to hazard a guess as to what they're doing."

"They are over there arguing whether to watch 'Wheel of Fortune', 'Roller Derby Mamas' or a Chinese Ping-Pong tournament," he gritted.

"Something tells me 'Roller Derby Mamas' will win."

"This is not a joke!" Tyler yelled.

Letitia covered her ears. "Do you mind? This room isn't very large and you have a very loud voice when your temper is showing."

"Dammit, Ticia, this is a working ranch, not a damn relaxation center!" He lowered his voice a fraction of a decibel. "Next thing I know, they'll spend all their time watching instead of working. And it's all your fault!"

"*My* fault? Why, because Jack is my brother and he thought he was doing something nice?" she shot back. "I'm sorry his idea backfired, but I am not taking the blame for it. I assume those men are all adults. They should know the difference between playtime and worktime."

Tyler shook his head. "You have to understand there isn't all that much to do out here and when winter comes there's days when no one goes outside unless they absolutely have to. This is like some new toy to them that they can't get enough of. I'm afraid I'm going to wake up one morning and find out they're not going outside until the morning game shows are over." His mouth twisted. "It's not as if I can put restrictions on it like they're a bunch of kids. So. *You're* the boss, *you* take care of it."

Letitia stood up. "All right, I'll take care of it," she repeated. "Fine. I'll do just that." She marched out of the office and down the hall.

"Oh hell," he groaned, already sensing her intent. "Where do you think you're going?"

"To take care of it as you suggested," she threw over her shoulder as she pulled open the front door and slammed it behind her.

"What have you done now?" Myrna looked up from her perch on the couch.

Tyler threw up his hands. "Pardon me for living!" he shouted, opening the door with a force that could have pulled it off its hinges. "I should have personally driven her back to Beverly Hills that first day! This place is going nuts!" The house shook when he slammed the door.

"Wish those two would just get together and be done with it," Myrna said to no one in particular, returning to her movie.

Tyler had to practically run to keep up with Letitia's rapid steps. "Look, I'm sorry I blew up."

She didn't look at him as she crossed the yard. "No, you're not."

"This is not going to work."

"Want to bet?" This time she shot him a sideways glance. "After all, betting is one of your strong points, isn't it?"

Tyler picked up his pace to head her off. He held his hands out. "No."

She stopped before she could run into him. "Don't worry, Tyler, I'll make it as painless as possible." She feinted to the left and the minute he moved, she swiftly shifted the other way and hurried up the steps to the bunkhouse.

Tyler closed his eyes and muttered a curse as he heard her open the door. The talk and laughter inside fell into abrupt silence.

Letitia's body standing in the doorway was illuminated by the light streaming outside.

"Missy, this isn't a good idea." J.T. was the first to break the silence.

Letitia looked across the room to the television screen. "I was right. 'Roller Derby Mamas' won," she said under her breath when Tyler came up behind her.

"Gentlemen—" she presented them with a bright smile "—Myrna asked that I remind you that she's making blueberry pancakes tomorrow for breakfast and she hopes no one will be coming in late. You know how she feels toward latecomers." She started to turn away then turned back as if she'd forgotten something. "Oh, and men, if you get hooked on that thing and your work suffers, I will send both satellite dishes back without a second thought. And believe me, I'm not a nice person to be around if I don't have my MTV," she said pleasantly. "Good night, gentlemen, pleasant dreams." She pulled the door closed. Her smile disappeared the moment she faced Tyler. "I hope that met with your approval."

"Now I know you're nuts." He followed her back to the house.

"It must have something to do with the company I keep." Letitia entered the house, almost closing the door in Tyler's face if he hadn't caught it in time.

"You think you can solve everything that easily?"

Letitia suddenly spun around. "No, but I do the best I can. And you could offer the use of your brain."

"Other than suggest you rob a bank? And I wouldn't be surprised if old man Beecham had poisonous snakes patrolling the bank after hours. What about your brother? If he's willing to give up an extra satellite dish, maybe he'd spring for the payment."

"No!" She stormed back into her office. Her jaw looked as firm as Mount Rushmore. "This is *my* problem and *I* will be the one to solve it."

"How? The ranch is hocked to the hilt," he said candidly, following her inside and leaning against the doorjamb. "You said Beecham has given you five days. Do you intend to go to L.A. or New York and charm a banker there? What are you going to offer for collateral? Yourself?" His voice rose with every word.

"If it became necessary and I thought it would help, I'd go to L.A. or New York and see bankers there for

business negotiations," she retorted. "But there are
other ways of handling this."

"Such as?" Tyler asked skeptically. He suddenly
snapped his fingers. "Oh, I know, you're going to get
proof your ex-husband is alive and well and hanging
out with Elvis, so you can get all your back alimony."

Letitia flexed her fingers, fully prepared to claw his
eyes out.

The sound of the telephone was the bell to end
round one. Letitia snatched up the receiver.

"Hello? Cecile, how *are* you?" Her voice brightened as she identified her caller. "Oh, everything is
fine. Are the cowboys as sexy as magazines try to say
they are?" She looked straight at Tyler and winked.
"Well, it depends on what you're looking for. There
are those who chew tobacco, scratch themselves, and
take a bath once a week." She laughed as she perched
her butt on the edge of the desk while keeping her gaze
focused on Tyler. She cocked her head to one side as
she listened to the caller. "Cute ones? Oh, there are a
few good-looking men, if you like the denim and boots
type."

Tyler stood there and saw a new side of Letitia. This
was the woman he thought he saw that first day. She
laughed, repeated snippets of gossip and chattered like
a lovely magpie. After about a half hour of what he
considered useless conversation, he noticed even her
stance changed.

"Why did I call you?" Letitia held one hand out in
front of her studying her nails. "It's this way. I've decided there's no use in keeping some of my jewelry out
here in the sticks. After all, I wouldn't have anywhere
appropriate to wear them. So I wondered if you could
give me the name of a reliable jeweler I could contact

to handle some of my pieces for sale." She sounded so casual that she could have been asking for the name of a good hairdresser. "What pieces am I considering giving up? Oh, I thought my emerald and diamond necklace and earrings to start, perhaps the gold swan pin studded with sapphires, my ruby pendant," she proceeded to name four other pieces of jewelry that sent Tyler's mind reeling. She wiggled her fingers at him. "My canary diamond ring?" She looked upward. "Well, to be honest, I hadn't thought about selling that piece. It was one of Stephano's last gifts to me and has a lot of sentimental value."

Tyler chuckled when Letitia pretended to stick her finger down her throat and crossed her eyes.

"Well, I had it appraised recently when the insurance renewed," she babbled on, quoting a figure that caused Tyler to choke. He wondered how people could throw around these high figures without fainting. "Well, I know you've always loved that ring, but you have to understand I can't let it go for anything lower than the appraisal figure. How would Evan feel about that? Oh, he did?" she bubbled. "No wonder you want the ring! All right, Cecile, I'll call Frank's office first thing in the morning and he'll contact you to arrange the sale. He has access to my safety deposit box and can give you the ring right away. No, darling, I won't back out on our agreement. As far as I'm concerned, verbal is as good as written. Yes, we must talk again. Bye, bye." She hung up.

"I've never heard a telephone conversation so obviously fake," Tyler told her. "I felt as if I was listening to some kind of talking plastic figurine. Still, that was one smooth piece of work you just accomplished. Slick. You weren't just calling her for the name of someone to handle your jewelry, were you?"

She shook her head, looking very pleased with herself. "If that's what I wanted, I could just call my attorney to handle it. She's been panting after that ring ever since the first time her avaricious beady eyes saw it. It was a custom design Stephano gave me a year before our divorce," she explained. "I'm truthfully not all that fond of it because it's too ostentatious for me, so I only wore it when I wanted to make a statement."

"The money you get from selling the ring will easily bring the loan up-to-date," he guessed.

She smiled and nodded. "With some left over."

His eyes seemed to be opening up more and more around her. It appeared she was willing to do whatever was necessary. "A lot of women wouldn't be willing to give up their jewelry to save a ranch. It's not something you have to do."

"Of course it is. The finances are my problem." She looked at him as if it couldn't be any other way.

His smile grew broader. The lady was most definitely getting to him. "You'll ruin Mr. Beecham's day. He lives to foreclose."

She laughed and threw her hands up. "That's show biz."

Tyler joined in her laughter as he grabbed her hands and pulled her toward him. "You are one cocky lady," he murmured.

"And you're the most exasperating man I have ever met and believe me, I've known more than my share," she stated, placing one hand against his chest. His body heat immediately wrapped itself around her fingers.

"Then we're even, aren't we?" He circled her wrist with his fingers. "If I had any brains at all, I'd run the other way."

"But?" she whispered.

"But I guess my best bet is to fight fire with fire." Tyler leaned even closer as if he was going to kiss her. Letitia's lips started to slightly part, anticipating his move. He halted short of her mouth. "Good night, countess. Pleasant dreams." He straightened up and walked down the steps.

Letitia watched him leave with a mixture of frustration and humor. With just a hint of anticipation for spice. She pressed her hand against the doorjamb, finding the wood still warm from Tyler's body. "You'll be back, cowboy," she murmured. "You'll be back."

TYLER LAY IN BED with his hands folded behind his head. There was no way he could sleep when every time he looked up at the ceiling all he could see was Letitia's face.

I should just crawl through her window late one night.

"I THOUGHT FOR SURE he'd show up tonight," Letitia muttered, pacing back and forth in front of her bed. The folds of her peacock blue silk chemise swirled around her thighs with each step she took.

Le Chat looked up from his nest in the middle of the tumbled covers and gave a mighty feline yawn before settling back to sleep. He couldn't have cared less if his least favorite person showed up.

Letitia froze when she thought she heard a sound near the front door. She strained her ears but heard nothing more.

She bent down in front of the mirror, fluffed her hair and licked her lips before returning to the bed. She tried sleeping without the covers, then with them. She settled for the latter. She dropped back against the pillows.

''Well, he still might show up.''

TYLER SNAPPED UPRIGHT in bed. ''The window!'' He turned his head and looked at the open window with its cotton curtains flaring slightly from the late-night breeze. The window was the only one on this side of the building. He could easily climb onto the overhang and jump down.

Tyler crept out of bed and hurriedly pulled on a pair of jeans. He didn't care if it was the middle of the night. He was so damned hard just thinking about Letitia, he just knew she was lying awake thinking about him.

He carefully lifted the window a few more inches, wincing as it squeaked a soft protest. He tensed, fearing someone might hear it. Convinced all was well, he draped his leg over the sill then the other and climbed out onto the sloping roof. He carefully made his way down to the gutter and jumped to the ground. Then swore long and hard under his breath when he realized in his hurry to go to Letitia, he'd forgotten to put on his boots and had landed on a small pile of rocks that dug painfully into his bare feet.

Still cursing under his breath, he gingerly walked toward Letitia's bedroom window and at the same time, kept a sharp eye out to make sure no one was up and about. With his luck, Myrna would come out of her cabin with a shotgun.

Tyler felt the thrill of victory when he reached the window undetected. He started to pull himself through when he realized it wasn't open far enough.

"Letitia," he hissed, staring at the swathed figure on the bed across the room. "Ticia!" He hesitated when he saw glowing yellow eyes peering at him from the middle of the bed.

Giving up on getting her attention, he grunted with effort as he tried to open her window farther. He grasped the window-sill and pulled himself up and over. He groaned as the sill dug into his middle.

"Damn, I should have tried one of the doors."

"Ticia." He kept his voice quiet so he wouldn't alarm her. Then raised it. She didn't stir. "Dammit, woman, wake up!" he finally ordered in a fit of frustration, shaking her bare shoulder.

She slowly rolled over and peered up at him through slitted eyes. Le Chat, angry at being disturbed, jumped off the bed and stalked out of the room with his tail held high.

"Tyler, you're late," she said in a slurred voice. "I expected you long ago. And now you're a dream."

He chuckled softly. "Baby, I'm here," he insisted, sitting on the edge of the bed. "I'm not a dream."

She licked her lips. "Yes, you are. But I understand." She started to roll over again, but Tyler stopped her by holding on to her shoulder.

"Well, countess, I guess there's only way one to prove to you I'm not a dream." He pulled her upright into his arms. The kiss Prince Charming awakened Sleeping Beauty with was nothing compared to the heated kiss Tyler used on Letitia.

Letitia stirred slightly. Maybe this wasn't a dream after all, her mind hazily told her. Maybe he finally had shown up! She opened her mouth to accept his tongue and curled her own around his. In her somnolent state she could feel his body heat radiating against her splayed palms, the crisp hairs on his chest prickling her fingertips. She rubbed a nipple to a tiny taut pebble. She felt herself falling backward against the pillows and his body following her down.

"Ticia, you better wake up soon," his husky voice crooned in her ear. "It would be a hell of a lot more fun if you actively participated."

"Mmm, I am awake," she murmured, enjoying what her hands were finding. A tiny frown furrowed her brow.

"Tyler?" Her voice was clearer this time, although her eyes still remained closed.

His lips nipped hers. "In the flesh, darlin'. Why don't you open your gorgeous eyes and take a look?"

She blindly groped. Her fingers encountered denim and bare hair-dusted flesh above that. She slowly opened one eye. Then the other. There was next to no light, but there was more than enough for her to identify her late-night visitor. She decided this was the perfect way to be awakened. Even in the middle of the night.

"What took you so long?"

Tyler's mouth dropped open. He chuckled. "Most women would scream if they found a man in their bedroom in the middle of the night."

She looped her arms around his neck and pulled him back down next to her. "I would have thought that by now you'd realize I'm not most women."

"And I'm damned glad." Tyler pushed the covers back. Sweat immediately broke out on his brow as he stared at the scrap of silk barely covering her body. "Lady, you sure know how to dress for bed, don't you?"

Letitia stretched under his admiring gaze. "Like it?"

"Too much." He couldn't stop staring at the peacock blue silk chemise that bared enough arm, chest and legs to send his blood pressure sky-high.

"It's a lot more practical than your idea of nightwear." She traced the jeans' metal button with her fingertip, then flicked it open. She slowly pushed the zipper downward. A sharp breath of air escaped her lungs when, instead of the opening revealing cotton fabric, she found dark coarse hair springing outward. "I've heard of cowboys sleeping with their boots on..."

"I sleep in the raw," he explained, his voice growing hoarse under her exploration.

"Yes, I see that." Her gaze slowly traveled upward with her mouth following. His flesh was warm and slightly salty. She impatiently pushed his jeans down his hips while he scrambled to help finish the task. Her chemise met with the same fate as their few pieces of clothing were tossed off the bed.

Letitia's neck bowed as Tyler traced every inch of her upper body with his hands and mouth. He nuzzled the hollow of her throat, all the while telling her exactly how he'd love her. She cried out in ecstatic agony as he nudged his knee between her parted thighs, giving her only partial satisfaction.

"Dreams are nothing compared to the real thing," she moaned. Her hands fluttered around him as he latched on to her nipple and sucked inward.

"I want you so much that I'm afraid it will be over before it really begins," he muttered hoarsely against her skin as he felt her breast swell under his touch.

Her breath caught in her throat as his sucking motion was felt all through her body. "Then we'll just have to try again, won't we?"

Tyler smoothed his hands down Letitia's body, enjoying the feel of her silky skin. She twisted and turned in his embrace, crying out as he traced patterns on her abdomen before venturing lower. The hair curled madly around his fingers as he found her center moist and welcoming. He tongued each rosy pink nipple to a tight peak.

"Letitia." All he could speak was her name as he rotated his palm against her, feeling her moist heat reach out to him. She twisted her body under the loving pressure.

"I need you," she breathed, grabbing hold of his arms and trying to pull him back down to her.

He started to pull away. "I need to get something out of my jeans."

She held on tight. "It's all right."

Tyler needed little encouragement. He rested his hips against hers, slowly thrusting down as her body arched up. He bared his teeth when her sheath enveloped him in a tender caress. He looked down and found her gazing up at him with the same look of awed wonder he knew had to be on his own face. He couldn't believe anything could feel so perfect. He pulled back and thrust again. He wanted to make it last forever. He cupped the back of her head in his palm, feeling her hair spill around his fingers in a tawny cloud as he lifted her face to his. They stared at each other, unable to say a word. None was needed as each silently telegraphed what they were experiencing at that moment. Still, keeping her eyes on his face, Letitia slowly raised one hand, brushing the damp hair away from Tyler's face. He took her hand and pressed his mouth against the palm. She kept her eyes open as his face grew nearer to hers.

He made love to her mouth with the same intensity another part of his body used to catch her up in a maelstrom of colors and sensations.

"Tyler!" Her nails raked his back as she seemed to draw him even deeper inside her. Her legs wrapped themselves tightly around his hips as if she couldn't bear to let him go.

"Stay with me, baby." His voice was raw, teetering on the brink of completion.

If Tyler could have had a coherent thought at that moment, he would have realized he'd found a perfect way to keep Letitia quiet. She was past any point of coherency.

The world seemed to erupt around her. Feeling as if she couldn't take it all in, Letitia sunk her teeth into Tyler's shoulder. The sharp pain was the only thing needed to send him hurtling over the edge with her.

TYLER ROLLED OVER on to his side and tucked Letitia against his chest. He took slow stock of his surroundings. The soft cotton beneath him, his head cradled by a firm pillow that smelled of Letitia, her skin damp against his. He wrapped his arms around her just below her breasts and kissed the top of her head.

"I see you believe in that hackneyed phrase," Letitia said quietly, with the faintest hint of amusement.

He couldn't remember the last time he'd ever felt this relaxed after making love. Or if he'd *ever* felt this way before. Something about her seemed to take him out of himself and wring him dry. He nibbled the soft skin behind her ear.

"What phrase are you talking about?"

She turned her head. Her breath wafted across his chest, cool on his sweat-slicked skin.

"Ride 'em cowboy."

Chapter Twelve

"How did the old goat take it when you handed him the check?"

"Just as I thought he would. His face turned so red that I thought he'd choke. He was doubly shocked that I came in a full twenty-four hours ahead of the deadline."

Tyler laughed at the picture Letitia drew. Uncaring who saw him, he grabbed her around the waist and twirled her in a circle.

"Tyler, put me down!" She laughed, holding onto his shoulders to balance herself.

He set her back on her feet but kept his hands on her waist. "I was wrong, countess," he said softly. "It appears you have more grit than I first thought. Amazing how one ring with a huge rock could do so much good."

"By the times the penalties were tabulated, there wasn't much left," she admitted. "And he enjoyed reminding me the due date for next quarter's payment. That will be here before I know it. But for now, I intend to do a little enjoying of my own." She looked around the center of town, her brain already racing with ideas.

Her exuberance left him feeling a bit wary. Letitia was well known for her larger than life ideas. "What are you cooking up now?"

"I wouldn't dream of inflicting my fledgling culinary skills on anyone just yet." She was so happy she wasn't going to take offense at his teasing remark. "But that isn't going to stop me from planning a party. I want to have a 'get to know Letitia DeMarco' party. We could have a barbecue and a band." She was already lost in her plans. "We could get a band, couldn't we?"

Tyler paused. He knew what kind of gossip had been roaming the county about her. So far, he'd been lucky enough to keep it from her. While the people hadn't been downright rude, they had been cautious and standoffish when they met up with her. He had to hand it to her. She always presented a smiling face and a warm manner and there were people she'd charmed. A charm he now knew was sincere. If only he could make the rest of them see her the way he did.

"Yeah, we could get a band. I know some men who play at church socials and such. They're pretty good."

The brightness in her eyes dimmed a little. "You don't look very happy about my idea. I thought it would be a good way for people to realize that I intend to stay here."

"It's going to take more than stopgap measures, Letitia," he said quietly. "You're going to have to start thinking about what you're going to do next. There's a lot of hard work ahead of you. If anyone knows, it's me."

"Well, that's obvious. I need to find a way to turn the ranch into a paying proposition," she answered without hesitation. "Any suggestions? After all, you want the ranch too. What would you do?"

"*Not* turn it into a dude ranch," he retorted.

She nodded. "Well, at least we know what *not* to turn it into." She sighed. "How about big-time cat breeders with Le Chat as our patriarch?"

"Try again," he suggested, opening the truck door for her.

"I want to stop by that bookstore we drove past," she decided.

"More reading material?"

She settled down in the seat. "In a way."

Letitia decided to hold off pursuing the subject until they left the bookstore where she'd picked up every ranching journal and magazine she could find. And laughed when Tyler chose the latest copy of *Popular Mechanics*.

"So, what plans did you have for the ranch?" she persisted, turning in the seat and leaning against the door. "Please Tyler, I really am interested."

He still hesitated. "I grew up in Idaho. My dad had a good-sized ranch, but he tried to build it up too fast and ended up losing it all. One thing I learned was what *not* to do in ranching. I want to start out small and build up slowly. My ultimate dream was to raise quarter horses. There was a rancher in Wyoming who had to slow down because of poor health. I heard about him through some friends. We talked a few times, but . . ." He shrugged it off.

She could sense his sorrow over what could have been an excellent chance for him. She also knew any show of sympathy would only cause his stubborn side to rear its ugly head again. Amazing what she had learned about him since that first time they made love.

It hadn't stopped their arguing at every other turn, but it had given them a new way to resolve their differences.

"I understand J.T. makes a belly-burning pot of chili. Do you think he'd make some for the barbecue?" Letitia wondered aloud.

By now, Tyler had grown used to the abrupt changes in subject. This time, he knew she did it for a good reason and silently blessed her for it. "All you'll have to do is bat those big beautiful eyes at him and he'll do anything you ask." His mouth moved in a crooked smile. "I'll expect you to dance every dance with me," he said gruffly.

"I beg your pardon?" She used her best upper-crust accent.

"You can beg it anytime you want."

"I don't believe in dancing with just anyone," Letitia haughtily informed him. "I will require a long list of references."

Tyler grinned. "What about my warm and wonderful personality? Doesn't that count?"

"Not if you think I'm going to let you dance all over my feet with those big boots of yours," she informed him.

"I thought bigger was better."

"Not in boots."

"My boots are special," Tyler told her.

Her gaze flickered downward but didn't quite make it as far as his boots. "It appears that's not all that's special."

He took several deep breaths, although by now he knew they wouldn't do a bit of good where Letitia was concerned. She always managed to keep him so off balance he wasn't sure if he was coming or going. The last week of getting little sleep hadn't helped either, but his nights in Letitia's bed were more than worth it. At least he'd sneaked in a ten-minute doze while waiting for her to finish her business in the bank. Right now, he just wanted to listen to her excitedly make plans for the party while they drove back to the ranch.

Letitia couldn't remember ever feeling so happy. And she knew Tyler had a great deal to do with it. The past week had been full of surprises when he'd crept through her bedroom window almost every night. The only dark spot was that he had to leave so he'd be back in his own bed when it was time to get up.

She wanted to tell him that this party was as much for him as for her. She hoped by meeting her neighbors in a social atmosphere, she would have a better chance of getting to know them. And for them to get to know her. While she was too busy to feel lonely she feared the day would come when she would crave other people to talk to. Women her own age. Besides, the ranch was her home now. She had a lot of plans for that, too.

Myrna was soon caught up in Letitia's excitement. She did her share of helping her plan the party and volunteered to make the calls. She also gently warned Letitia.

"You have to realize that a lot of people move out here from the city. When they discover the isolation and the hard life, they pack up and move away. That's why so many are wary of making friends." The two women worked companionably in the kitchen baking cakes and pies for the barbecue as Letitia mulled over the work.

"I do not intend to move away," she said firmly, grimacing at the mangled pie crust she'd been rolling

out. Myrna made it look so simple. She couldn't remember the last time she'd been so excited about entertaining. "This is my home now. It took a gun for
me to get this land, so I don't intend to let it go easily."

"And the next quarter's payment on the loan?"
Myrna asked bluntly, as she pulled round cake pans
out of the oven.

"Once the rest of my jewelry is sold, I can easily pay
it and have money to put away." Letitia absently
scratched her nose, leaving a white dot of flour on the
tip.

"You can't give it *all* up, child. It isn't right."

"Women gave up a great deal more when they first
homesteaded here. They left behind their family, lost
children, sometimes husbands, and discarded personal items just to keep going."

Myrna shook her head. "I thought you promised to
quit watching those movies and accepting them as
gospel."

Letitia wrinkled her nose at the woman's gentle
chiding. "This one about moving west was interesting. Besides, from those movies I did learn enough not
to suggest we run sheep."

"Sheep!" Tyler walked in on the tail end of the
conversation. "Them's fightin' words." He flicked the
tip of her nose and showed her the white smudge on
his fingertip.

"Yes, I found that out in an Errol Flynn movie.
Still, I intend to come up with an excellent way to
make this ranch pay for itself," she insisted.

"I can't wait to see what you come up with," he told
her as he swiped a cookie off the cooling rack and got
the back of his hand smacked with Myrna's spoon.

"Just about every one of you men have been in here today on one excuse or another to steal my cookies," she said sternly. "At this rate, there won't be any cookies left and none of you will be hungry enough to eat that meal I've been fixing."

Tyler grabbed her playfully around the waist. "Only because no one can bake them like you, Myrna, my love," he crooned, dancing her around the kitchen and stopping to bend her over his arm in a dip worthy of Fred Astaire.

Letitia stopped her task and watched them. She couldn't remember the last time she saw Tyler's eyes as the cold gray stones she'd seen in the beginning. So much had happened since then that she didn't feel like the same person. Even Jack, in Letitia's last phone call to her brother, commented on how relaxed she sounded instead of a frenetic woman on a merry-go-round.

She looked down at her flour-covered jeans and cotton shirt. No wonder she didn't feel the same. She wasn't. She clapped her hands several times over her head. "All right, you two, dance class is over. You did very well today. Next week, we will work on the tango."

Tyler grinned. "Didn't you get any cookies to sweeten your disposition, countess?"

She held up the rolling pin. "I'm not allowed to graduate to cookie baking until I master the pie crust." She brandished it threateningly when Tyler strolled over to take a closer look. "If you say one word, you will have a permanent dent in your rock-hard skull."

He studied the dough that looked as if it had been handled too many times. "What kind of pie?"

She eyed him suspiciously. "Lemon meringue."

"I want the first piece," he mock whispered before leaving.

"It's not just any man who's willing to eat the first piece of your pie when he's never eaten your cooking before," Myrna advised.

Letitia roused herself. She feared she looked like a love-starved teenager. "I don't know what you mean." She affected bland innocence.

"Yes, you do. Just don't think others aren't noticing the way he looks at you and you look at him." Myrna shook her head. "Some days the way you two look at each other practically starts a brush fire."

"We've just getting along better, that's all."

Myrna chuckled. "So that's what you call it now."

"LETITIA. LETITIA. Dammit, if you fall asleep again I will toss you into an ice-cold shower to wake up your sorry hide."

"How barbaric can you get, Tyler Barnes," she scolded, hurrying into the bedroom from the bathroom. She bent at the waist and rested her elbows on the windowsill. "What's up?" She wiggled her eyebrows. "Besides you, that is."

Tyler shook his head. "Get dressed."

"Why? Is there something wrong with what I'm already wearing?" Letitia straightened up and stood back to show him a black silk floor-length nightgown. What boosted Tyler's blood pressure were the sheer panels set in strategic areas clearly meant to fire up a man's imagination. "If so, I can take it off." She lifted her hands to the narrow straps.

Tyler groaned. "I love it, but I don't think you'll want to wear it in the barn."

"Are we talking about that roll in the hay you promised me?" She looked hopeful.

"Just get dressed in something you don't care if it gets dirty and come on out to the barn," he told her. He disappeared from the window before she could question him further.

"This better be good," she muttered, changing into jeans and a sweatshirt and pulling on her boots.

When Letitia entered the barn, she heard muted voices coming from the other end of the building where a light shone.

"Think it's going to be much longer?" Tyler's voice came out loud and clear.

"Shouldn't be," J.T. replied. "I'd say within the next hour or so."

Letitia walked quietly toward the voices. "What's going on?" she asked softly then stopped short when she saw the men crouched down in a stall calming a restive pregnant mare. Her eyes widened in wonder. "Is she going to have her baby?"

Tyler nodded. "We've been waiting for Lady Anne to foal for the past week. She never likes to keep a schedule the way the other mares do. She's ornery—" his gaze swept upward to enfold Letitia "—like someone else I know."

Letitia crouched down next to him. "Shouldn't the vet be here?" she whispered, unable to keep her eyes off the straining mare.

"I wouldn't worry, missy. I was bringing foals into the world before you were born," J.T. informed her as he stroked the mare's quivering flanks. "She's going to be just fine. This isn't Lady Anne's first, so she knows what to do. Don't ya, girl?" he crooned to the mare who lifted her head and nickered in response.

"Letitia, will you go into the tack room and get us some more towels, please?" Tyler asked. "They're kept in a plastic bag marked Maternity."

"Would it help if I boiled some water?"

The two men exchanged smiles.

"No, just the towels, please," Tyler answered.

She slowly backed out of the stall then ran for the supplies he requested and ran back, only slowing down when she reached the stall. "Here." She held out the packet.

"Tyler! Come around here and help!" J.T. looked up.

Letitia sat down cross-legged with her back against the wall. She watched a miracle as the men assisted the tiny foal into the world, carefully pulling two tiny legs out.

"Is it all right?" she whispered, watching them clear the mouth and nostrils of mucus. She was so enthralled with the beauty the sight of blood and birth fluids didn't repulse her. All she saw was a new baby and it sent signals deep down inside her body that she'd never felt before.

"He's just fine." Tyler looked up with a smile then froze as he saw the beauty shining in her face and eyes. He stared at her glowing features and wondered *is this how she'd look if she just had our child? She's so beautiful to begin with, but I want to see her with our baby.* He felt the emotions slamming into his gut like a sledgehammer.

This is what real life is like, Letitia thought with wonder. *This is what I want with Tyler.* She blinked rapidly to keep the tears back. "He's so tiny," she said in a choked voice, watching the foal struggle to his feet, his long legs wobbly as he headed directly for his mother.

"You wait and see. He'll grow to be as big as his daddy," J.T. predicted. He looked from Letitia to Tyler and smiled. "Tyler, why don't you see Letty back to the house? I'll keep watch the rest of the night. Although I doubt they'll need me." He watched the newborn colt with pride.

Tyler got to his feet and walked over to Letitia. He held out his hand, which she accepted and allowed him to pull her upright. Still in awe of what they just witnessed and what they just experienced between each other, they were silent as they walked toward the back door. Just before he opened it, Letitia stopped him.

"Look." She turned and pointed upward. "Do you think there's a new star up there for him?"

"The way I heard it, there's a new star when people die," Tyler said quietly.

She shook her head. "Oh, no, stars are for new babies. Stars celebrate life, not mourn it. See!" She gleefully pointed toward a shooting star. "That's his. He's now official."

Tyler wrapped his arms around her waist and pulled her back against him with his cheek resting on top of her head.

"You're still trying to live a fairy-tale life, countess," he murmured.

She rested her hands on top of his, right now content to feel his body against hers as they shared these quiet moments. "Not anymore. I'm not looking for that magic castle in the sky or that knight on the white horse to save me from the fiery dragon. But you know what would be nice?"

"What?" His voice was muffled as he nuzzled her ear.

"I know you should probably get back to the bunkhouse, but I wish you could come in and just hold me for a little while." She turned her head to press her cheek against his chest.

Without saying a word, Tyler turned her around and picked her up in his arms. He shouldered the door the rest of the way open and carried her into the bedroom where he set her down on the tumbled covers as carefully as if she was a piece of rare china. He silently removed her clothing and tucked her under the covers. "I'm going to take a quick shower," he told her.

She smiled and caressed his cheek. "I'll be here."

He nodded. He started to straighten up then paused. He looked back down at her with a strange look on his face. He framed her face with his hands and brushed a gentle kiss against her lips.

"Do you realize how special you are?" he whispered.

"It's always nice to hear," her voice broke.

"Then expect to hear it often." With that, he headed for the bathroom.

Letitia smiled as she watched him leave the room. She curled up on her side cradling her pillow between her arms as she listened to the shower running. Tyler noticed the light in her eyes when he returned with a towel wrapped around his hips and another in his hand as he dried his hair. Letitia smiled.

"I've never seen anything born before," she said quietly. "It was so beautiful."

"It happens around here a lot, but we try not to take it for granted. Hey, move over." He smiled as he nudged her with his hip. He lifted the covers and slid in beside her. The moment he pulled her into his arms, he felt as if all was right with the world.

"Things happen so fast that sometimes we forget to slow down and cherish them," Letitia murmured. "I don't want to forget anything. I want to wrap all these memories up in tissue paper and keep them forever."

Tyler experienced a sharp pang of fear. "You sound as if you're taking off for parts unknown tomorrow."

She shook her head. Tyler felt her hair brush across his face, several strands clinging to his mouth. He could smell the lingering faint floral scent of her shampoo. Nothing else could be so arousing.

"You, of all people, know how outspoken I can be," she began.

His chuckle rumbled deep in his chest. "I'd say I've had some experience with that side of you, yes."

"Then you'll understand this." Her quiet voice floated in the night air. "I don't want it to end, Tyler. I'm probably a fool for saying it out loud, but I need to. I need to tell you how I feel." She turned in his arms, so she could see his face. And his reaction. "Call it one of my weaknesses. You mean a lot to me."

He held her so tightly that she could barely breathe. "Do you realize what gift you've just given me?" he asked hoarsely, burying his face against the curve of her neck.

"Is it of some value?"

"Definitely."

She felt a warmth radiate outward from her heart at his reply and the security of his arms surrounding her. "I'm glad."

"I'd say this has taken us another step," he murmured, using his nose to nuzzle her hair away from her cheek.

She wanted to burst out in song. Except she sang just as badly as Tyler did. She settled for slipping her arms around his neck. "I'd say so."

"So, countess. Wanna go a little bit farther?"

"What do you have in mind?"

He nudged his knee between hers.

"I guess we'll have to play it by ear and see what we can come up with, won't we?"

She shifted her body until she could easily take him in. "I don't think I need to worry. After all, you always manage to come up with something."

Their loving was slow and easy as they took their time to savor all the nuances. They touched softly, slowly, kissed any spot of skin they could find, murmuring words of praise for each other, telling each other what they liked, showing the same. This time, their loving climaxed in something so wondrous, so joyful, they couldn't have described what had happened between them if they'd tried to. It was just as meaningful as the first time they'd made love.

Letitia stirred when Tyler left the bed about an hour later. She immediately slid over until she lay cradled on his side where she could curl up with his pillow. Her eyes were at half mast as she watched him dress.

"Tyler." Her voice was rusty with sleep.

He paused in zipping his jeans and sat down on the bed. "What?" He carefully brushed a lock of hair away from her eyes and kept his fingers cupping her cheek.

"You said we need to take things a bit further?" Her sleepy smile hit him as hard as her kisses did. All he could think of was climbing back in that bed and burying himself in her sweet body that drew him in so lovingly. He knew he'd never wanted a woman as badly as he wanted Letitia. No other woman gave to him what she did so freely. And he cherished her gifts.

He laughed softly. "Yeah."

She snuggled down in his pillow, glorying in his scent embedded in the soft cotton. "Well, I hate to tell you this, but this isn't any ordinary relationship we have here."

He dropped a kiss on her lips. "For a woman who can usually think on her feet, you sure can be slow at times."

Chapter Thirteen

"I can't believe how festive it all looks. The men did a wonderful job of setting everything up." Letitia looked around the yard decorated with colorful hanging lights among the trees. The men had also sectioned off one section of the yard to be used as a dance floor with an upraised wooden stand for the band. Letitia and Myrna were busy covering the long tables set off to one side with brightly colored cloths and bringing out plates, cups, utensils and stacks of napkins.

"You know, usually my job in setting up a party was checking to make sure everything was in order," Letitia explained to Myrna. "Actually getting in and fixing food and setting tables is much more fun."

The older woman smiled her understanding. "Only because you feel as if it's all your own." Letitia looked over at the large pit the men had dug earlier. She could smell the spicy barbecued beef that permeated the air from the pit J.T. presided over with the importance of a world-famous chef.

"There hasn't been a party here in years. Harvey wasn't into socializing too much," Myrna told her. "The men were looking forward to this get-together so much, they were happy to do the heavy work." She clucked her tongue as she looked Letitia over from head to toe. "I'd say if you intend to play hostess you better think about cleaning yourself up. Right now, you look more like a kitchen maid than the lady of the house."

Letitia grimaced at her shorts and cotton top, which were stained with barbecue sauce, a few suspicious grease stains and a few other unidentifiable spots. "At least I have proof I did my part in all this." She glanced at the clock and imagined the hands were racing around the face at breakneck speed.

"You go on inside and take a long bath and put on your prettiest outfit," Myrna suggested, ushering her back to the house. "You may as well know now that some of these people are coming because they're curious to meet Running Springs' new owner. You want them to see how well you've settled in."

Letitia groaned. She hated feeling as if she was on trial. "So I guess that means I shouldn't serve the French champagne and Beluga caviar before we feast on that cow we cooked," she quipped.

"We barbecued a side of beef," she corrected.

"Same thing."

"Not exactly." Myrna gave her a gentle push. "Off with you. Get yourself pretty for Tyler."

Letitia shot her an innocent look that was so bland it could have doubled as vanilla pudding. Except Letitia couldn't be bland no matter how hard she tried. "Why just for Tyler? There're going to be other eligible men here tonight."

The older woman's smile was all knowing. "Probably because he'll be the one to appreciate your efforts the most. And I think he's the only one who counts in your eyes."

Letitia leaned forward to confide, "You know what, Myrna? I think we should find a good-looking man for you, so you won't worry about everyone else."

She hooted at the idea. "Before you think about marrying me off, I suggest you learn more about cooking."

She shook her head, her braid swaying against her shoulders. "If the men thought I was going to do the cooking, any one of them would offer to marry you right off. I guess I could pair you up with J.T."

"And put up with his disgusting habit of chewing tobacco? No thank you!" She swatted the younger woman with a towel as Letitia ran laughing into the house.

Letitia quickly undressed and ran her bathwater. While waiting for the tub to fill, she smoothed on a soothing clay face mask. She settled in the hot water laced with her favorite bath oil. She rested her head against the porcelain rim and closed her eyes, content to breathe in the scented air and relax.

"Now, there's a picture to behold."

She opened her eyes. She wasn't surprised to find Tyler standing in the bathroom doorway.

"Hi there," she said in her best come-hither voice. "Care to join me?"

His lips twitched as if he couldn't hold back his laughter. "No thanks. I don't think the men would understand why I smell like a French whorehouse."

She lazily extended her leg out of the water and admired the way the water trickled down her calf. A quick glance assured her Tyler was doing the same.

"Are you trying to say I smell like a French whore-house?"

"You can get away with it better than I can."

She shot him a coy look. "Oh, come on."

He looked upward, concentrating on the ceiling as if something fascinating was up there. Letitia noticed his throat muscles worked rapidly.

"No offense, countess, but I don't think that stuff covering your face is right for my skin type." He flicked his fingers against his forehead in a salute and walked out.

Letitia leaned forward, convinced she could hear him laughing. As she leaned back, she caught her reflection in the mirror tiles she'd applied to the opposite wall. A shriek escaped her lips before she could stop herself. While she'd acted like this year's sex symbol to Tyler, her face had been covered with the dark gray-green mask except for circles around her eyes, nose and mouth. She absently rubbed her hands against her cheeks, smearing the thick goo on her fingers.

"Perhaps I should just go ahead and drown myself."

"TALK ABOUT MIRACLES," Tyler murmured in Letitia's ear. "I thought you were trying a new makeup technique. I'm glad to see you decided against it. Take it from me, the natural look is more you."

She wrinkled her nose. "You enjoyed that, didn't you?" She fingered the soft gray shirt that matched his eyes. The shirt and dark gray twill dress slacks created a more sophisticated look for the man, although Letitia would have considered him fantastic no matter what he wore.

He shrugged. "Everything but your face." His gaze slid over her off-white lace trimmed camisole that topped a violet-sprigged front-buttoned full skirt. She'd left five buttons near the hem unbuttoned to reveal a lace-trimmed petticoat that matched her top. She had pulled her hair back from the sides and tied it in loose curls. He ached to kiss the deep rose lipstick from her mouth and pick her up and carry her back into the house where they could be alone. Then he could start weaving patterns on the bare skin her top revealed just before he released every one of those tiny little buttons down the front. It would take him forever, but he knew the wait would be more than worth it. As a result, he was already counting the hours until the party finished and he could be alone with her. But given these people didn't get a lot of chances to socialize, this party could last far into the night.

"Any complaints on the footwear?" she teased, holding out a dainty foot shod in delicate lilac leather ballet-style slippers.

He shot her a telling look. "No comment." He suddenly stiffened. His curse was soft and decidedly unfit for mixed company.

"What's wrong?" Letitia grabbed his arm. "Tyler?"

He inclined his head downward. She looked down to see Le Chat, complete with lilac collar, up on his haunches while his front claws were buried deeply in Tyler's leg.

"Get...him...off...me...now," he said between whitened lips.

"Le Chat, that's a bad kitty," she crooned, bending down and carefully loosening each claw. The cat stared at her as if to say "Back off, Mom, he deserves this."

"Tyler, I am very sorry about this." She cradled the cat in her arms. "I told you he holds a grudge."

"He should have forgotten by now." He shook his leg to make sure it was all right.

"Not Le Chat. His memory is better than an elephant's. And once he has a vendetta against someone, he'll bide his time and get even every chance he gets. I'd watch out from now on."

He glared at the cat who seemed to look at him with feline loathing in his eyes. "I will not apologize to him," he gritted.

"It won't help. Le Chat doesn't believe in apologies."

Undaunted, Tyler bent down and deliberately stuck his face close to the cat's. "Maybe I should find me an old guitar. One that needs new cat gut strings."

Le Chat's eyes narrowed as he hissed at the man and lifted a front paw in warning.

"All right, children." She carried Le Chat to the back door and urged him inside. "Tyler, you are just as bad as he is."

"He started it."

Letitia looked out where she could see headlights bouncing down the road toward the house. She took several deep breaths to calm her nervous stomach.

"Hey, this is nothing new for you." Tyler noticed her agitation and sought to calm her. "Parties are a way of life for you."

"But they were never as important as this one," she said softly with great feeling. "I've never felt I've had to prove myself the way I do tonight."

He knew if there wasn't the many eyes on them, he would have kissed her until she forgot about her worries. "Just relax and enjoy yourself. You'll do fine." When two trucks stopped nearby, he nudged her forward and walked behind her to help greet the first guests.

All too soon, Letitia's head whirled with names and faces as people seemed to arrive in an endless stream. Luckily, her days as a champion party giver helped her in keeping the two together. She was grateful for Tyler staying by her side and smoothing over the bumpy spots that occasionally cropped up.

"I hear you plan to fix up the house next," Paula commented, looking around. Her manner to Letitia was stiff and smile faint, but Letitia considered it an accomplishment that she was talking to her.

Letitia's smile felt frozen in place. She wondered what it would take to break down this woman's self-inflicted barrier. "Yes, I thought painting the outside would make a world of difference," she said brightly. "Then I hope to work on the interior with paint and wallpaper. It will all take time, but I don't mind."

"So you plan to stay?"

She blinked at the woman's blunt challenging statement. "Of course, I do. This is my home now."

Paula gazed at Letitia's outfit. While her own skirt and off-the-shoulder top were similar in style, the difference in quality of fabric were easily apparent. "This isn't New York or Beverly Hills, Mrs. DeMarco. I heard you spent a lot of years in Europe. It's not easy to understand why you'd want to live here in Montana. You'll probably change your mind when winter comes."

Her aqua gaze didn't waver. "Call me Letitia, please."

Paula sipped from the cup of beer she held. "I just find it hard to believe you would want to live here after all those other places you've lived in."

"Believe me, Paula, it's not all that it's cracked up to be," she said quietly, turning her head when she heard Myrna call her name. "Would you excuse me, please?"

Letitia breathed a sigh of relief as she left the woman and made her way through the small crowd.

"Don't worry about Paula." Myrna easily read her harried expression and confided, "It's a sad fact, but she hasn't been happy living here for quite some time. She wants to move to a larger town, but ranching is all her husband knows. And it's his whole life. Just give her time. She'll come around."

She nodded. "Time is something I have plenty of."

"Well, good evening, little lady, I understand you're Running Springs' new owner." Letitia jumped as the man's voice sounded like a sonic boom behind her.

She quickly turned, forcing a smile on her lips. She held out her hand. All she could see was a large man running more to fat than muscle in a maroon shirt with string tie and silver bull's head tie slide. A matching buckle dominated his belly. She heard Myrna's soft groan and comment: "Oh no, I thought he was still in Cheyenne and wouldn't make it back in time." It was enough to tell her this visitor wasn't exactly a welcome one but the kind you can't ignore, either.

"Yes, I'm Letitia DeMarco."

"Cal Danvers. I own the Diamond Trey spread." He grabbed her hand between his two moist ones and pumped it down with a shoulder-jarring action. "I've

been on a buying trip in Cheyenne for the past week.
Wouldn't have been back if my stomach hadn't acted
up again. Can't eat what I used to. They said you were
a looker and they were right. Well, hell, girl, you belong in New York City not out here! You're a little
thing, ain't ya?'' He grinned and talked around a cigar clamped firmly between his teeth. He looked over
her shoulder the entire time he spoke. ''Fred! Fred!
You gotta hear this joke I heard at the auction!'' He
boomed. ''S'cuse me, someone I need to talk to. Nice
meetin' you, little lady.'' He cruised by.

''Who was that?'' Letitia asked, still keeping her
smile firmly fixed on her lips as she turned to Myrna.

''One of the richest and most boorish men in the
state, if not the entire country,'' she said quietly. ''He
owns more acreage than he knows what to do with and
some say has more money than God. Except he
belches, smokes those disgusting cigars everywhere, is
obnoxious, has somehow managed to go through
seven wives, who probably only married him for his
money, although I know I would have more taste, and
good sense, than that.''

A warm hand suddenly settled on her nape in a
comforting caress. ''Come on, countess, I'm claim-
ing our dance,'' Tyler said quietly in her ear. He slid
his hand down her bare arm until his fingers laced
through hers. He led her over to the dance floor which
was already crowded.

''I don't know these steps,'' she confessed.

''Don't worry, they're easy to follow,'' he assured
her, grabbing hold of her other hand and drawing her
close to him. ''I see you met Cal.''

She wrinkled her nose. ''I dread to think what he
uses instead of tobacco in those horrible smelly ci-

gars.'' She buried her nose against his shirtfront, inhaling the clean scent of his skin to chase away the stench of Cal's cigars.

Tyler bent his head to whisper in her ear, "He claims they're imported."

Letitia shook her head. "Not from any halfway civilized country."

"Hey Tyler, you going to share?" one of their neighbors kidded, tapping him on the shoulder.

Tyler didn't want to give her up. "Considering it's you Clint, I guess I can." He mustered up a smile as he relinquished Letitia who mouthed the word "coward" to him.

After that, Letitia barely made it around the dance floor once before she got a new partner.

Tyler stood off to one side, watching Letitia laugh and talk to her varied partners.

"It looks like she just might make it, after all," he said under his breath.

"You couldn't get the lady to come in for dress boots?" Rance demanded, walking up and slapping Tyler on the back. "You let her wear those little slippers in public?"

"There's no stopping her," he replied, turning to his friend. "How ya doing?"

"Just fine. You got quite a crowd here." Rance looked around.

Both men looked over when Cal boomed, "All right, little lady, let's show them some real stompin'!" He took up Letitia's hands and led her around the floor in a heavy-footed dance that matched his heavy-handed manner. Letitia looked like a mouse being pawed by a baboon.

Tyler sighed. "She doesn't look happy."

Rance chuckled. "Would you? You know, I'm pretty tolerant of people, but Cal is difficult to get along with."

"Difficult?" One man stopped as he heard the comment. "Cal has the manners of a rogue bull."

"Along with the dancing feet of one," Tyler said wryly, inwardly wincing when he noticed Cal's big foot trod on Letitia's toes. He gave her credit for not hauling off and letting him have it.

"Darlin', you dance like a feather!" Cal's loud voice easily carried. Letitia looked as if her weak smile was the best she could do. She craned her head around Cal's beefy shoulder and noticed Tyler standing on the sidelines. She shot him a look that ordered him to rescue her.

Rance chuckled and quickly looked down, pressing his fingers against his mouth. "Glad to see people were smart to wear my boots to this shindig."

Tyler looked off into the distance. He didn't like Cal any more than most people did, but he figured Letitia might as well find out the good and the bad to ranch ownership. "They wouldn't dare not wear them."

"Except the lady." Rance's laughter boomed upward from his chest. He looked toward the dance floor. "Think I'll cut in and save the lady from being crippled. If she isn't going to wear my boots, the least she can do is dance with me."

"She might think she didn't have it so bad with him once she has those monster feet of yours stomping on hers," Tyler retorted.

Rance shook his head as he made his way through the dancing couples. Tyler remained where he was, watching Rance tap Cal on the shoulder and quickly step in his place. Letitia looked up and laughed at something Rance said to her. As Tyler watched her face light up, he felt that hot burst of jealousy deep within him. Straightening his shoulders, he made his way toward them.

"Thought I'd collect my woman," he informed Rance in a mock-macho cowboy voice, stepping between them.

As the music slowed, Letitia looped her arms around his neck. She tipped her head back to have a better view of his face.

"It's about time."

He grinned. "Sore feet?"

"I think at least ten bones in each foot are broken," she confided, enjoying the brush of his body against hers. "No one warned me dancing could be so dangerous."

He held her even closer against him. "Then you should stick to better dancers."

She cringed when Cal's earthshaking laugh assaulted her ears.

"Don't tell me, he's always the last to leave," she moaned.

"Always."

"You could have lied."

The rest of the evening turned into a haze for Letitia. She later recalled eating some of the spicy barbecued beef with the Turners and the Wyatts, learning both families had been ranching the land for several generations.

"Vern really thinks llamas are better as pack animals than mules?" Cal's deep voice echoed across the crowd. "The man needs a good old-fashioned talking to! Let me tell you..." Letitia tuned out his rumble as he expounded on his favorite subject—himself as the all-time expert on any form of ranching.

She allowed Rance to tease her choice of footwear and promised to stop by for a pair of dress boots in the near future.

She sipped a glass of beer while listening to the Barretts tell her their plans to expand their quarter-horse operation within the next year and brag about their champion stallion the way parents brag about their children.

While sitting out a few dances she heard the Jamisons discuss with another couple their reasons for bringing in another breed of cattle to mix in with what they currently ran on their land in hope of improving their herd and increasing their future profit margin with the new breed.

"They're called Watusi cattle?" Letitia looked confused. "I thought they were a tribe. A human tribe."

Marian Jamison beamed as she nodded and replied, "They're cattle too. African Ankola Watusi cattle, actually. Perfect for crossbreeding. Their beef has half the cholesterol, they're disease resistant and can go up to twenty days without water."

Letitia nodded, although she was frantically trying to understand the technical terms the woman was throwing out with ease. "How wonderful," she murmured, wishing she could take notes.

"We were pleased," she stated. "We've been able to obtain top sperm too."

Letitia blinked, hoping she could match the other woman's enthusiasm on the subject and fearing she was failing miserably. She was trying so hard to be a part of this group, but she didn't realize bull sperm was such a hot topic! She assumed her facial mask was still in place since Marian didn't seem to think anything was wrong. "I guess that's good?"

"Good?" Cal Danvers appeared behind them. Marian looked as pained as Letitia felt. "Little lady, Marian would be talking grade A here. If you're going to inseminate, you want the best sperm you can get. Now, if you decide to go that route, you let me know.I can put you in touch with the right people." He waved his beer bottle in an arc. "You want to do this, darlin', you gotta do it right. You want it fresh, which is always better than frozen, you understand. Don't worry, it's always sent by overnight mail."

Letitia bit down on her lower lip, hard. She was so afraid of bursting into hysterical laughter at the idea of receiving a shipment of bull sperm by mail. What helped her remain straight-faced was realizing her previous social group probably discussed subjects this group would find funny.

"Helping's what neighbors are for, dear." Marian patted her hand, before moving on after glaring at Cal's back.

"'Course, you bein' a woman and all, you shouldn't have to worry about these things," Cal went on, his barrel chest rippling like a large bowl of maroon jelly. "But don't you worry, sweetheart, Cal can take care of anything you need." His smile wasn't lascivious, but it irritated her anyway.

It took all of her self-control to smile. "Thank you for your offer, Mr. Danvers, but I'm doing quite well, thank you."

"Now, now," he patted her shoulder with a ham sized hand. "Don't be shy."

"The last thing I would call myself is shy," she inserted.

"'Course not!" He laughed. "But there's some things you women just shouldn't worry about which is why we men are here to help out." He beamed, certain he was right. He waved his noxious cigar around. "I mean, look at you. Fancy clothes, delicate skin. You're used to an easier way of life, Miz DeMarco. To those salons where you pay a lot of money for a haircut and have your face worked on with expensive creams made from monkey glands or whatever. This is all new to you. You need someone to make sure you don't make a mistake."

"Oh, oh," Tyler breathed, recognizing the storm signals brewing in Letitia's eyes.

"As long as I'm the owner, Mr. Danvers, *I* will worry about *my* business," she firmly stated.

"Now honey, don't take it the wrong way," he said with a chuckle.

"No," she replied keeping her voice quiet but twice as firm. "Not darlin', not honey, not sweetie and especially not *little lady*." She bit each word out with stark precision. "My name is Letitia, Ticia or Mrs. DeMarco. Those are the only ones I answer to. Mr. Danvers, Cal, I am sure you are a very nice and caring man, but you seem to like to take it to the extreme. Well, I'll be honest. I *don't* like the way you act and if these good people were honest, they would say the same thing." She swept her arm in a half circle. "You come in here and tell people how they should be running their ranches. No one wants to be told what to do. I certainly don't. Now, I suggest you think about that and consider changing parts of your personality. Along with getting rid of those obnoxious cigars!'' She stabbed his chest with her forefinger. ''Perhaps if you turn into a real person, people won't avoid you. Basically, it's this. Behave yourself or else.''

Cal looked at her with such a stunned expression that Tyler almost burst out laughing. He knew that pole-axed expression only too well.

''Well, then, I'll say good night,'' Cal said stiffly before leaving.

Letitia watched the large man walk directly toward a shiny silver Cadillac convertible.

''Now, why doesn't that surprise me?'' she murmured.

''A lot of us have wanted to tell Cal off, but we just weren't sure what words to use,'' Marian told her. ''You did it just right.''

''I didn't want to be rude,'' she explained.

The older woman smiled. ''You weren't. I just wish it had been done a lot sooner.''

Everyone pretty much said the same thing as they later left after saying it was the best party they'd attended in a long time. Letitia was also invited to a variety of functions for the next few months.

''Have fun?'' Tyler appeared beside her.

''I've learned some interesting things.'' Letitia watched the last of her guests leave. She sighed and leaned against Tyler's side. ''I feel as if my entire body has been run through an old-fashioned wringer. Even my face hurts,'' she groaned, resting her cheek against his shoulder. ''And my feet are killing me! Myrna, don't bother cleaning anything up tonight. I'll help you in the morning when I've regained life.''

''I thought you were an international hostess,'' she teased. ''This should have been a snap for you.''

"Mainly sit-down dinners and cocktail parties before the opera or theater openings. Stephano's mother thrived on party planning and I let her do most of the work. Still, tonight was fun. More fun than any party I've been to before." She flexed her toes inside the soft leather slippers.

"Why don't you go on in?" Tyler gently pushed her down onto one of the benches while he checked the barbecue pit to make sure the coals were properly extinguished.

"It went well, didn't it?" Letitia felt her energy level start to rise again. "People were so nice and friendly. And they seemed to really enjoy themselves, too. I couldn't believe they were so open in talking about what they've done to keep their ranches going."

Tyler grinned. "They enjoy sharing their successes and complaining about their failures. Did you get some ideas, countess?"

She nodded, preferring to ignore the nickname. In fact, she was finally getting used to it. She also hoped if she stopped frowning at him every time he called her that he'd get bored and stop. "Except I can't do the same thing they're doing. We need something new. Otherwise we'll just be in the same fix we are now. No, we need to find a ranching method that will turn it into a profit-making machine. I don't expect anything world shattering, just something perfect for us."

He chuckled and shook his head in wonderment. "You're determined to figure something out to save the day, aren't you?"

Her smile reached out to him with warming fingers. "You bet your boots I do. Or we can start a betting pool and see who can come up with the perfect save-the-ranch plan first." She stifled a jaw-breaking yawn. "Although I'll be honest with you. I know it's a way of life out here and you all are used to just calling up and ordering sperm, but I don't know if it's ever anything I can do with a straight face. I guess it's something I'll have to work on," she mused, looking around with slightly glassy eyes that showed just how tired she was.

Tyler and Myrna exchanged confused frowns. Tyler thought for a moment then nodded and mouthed "the Jamisons." Myrna's mouth rounded in a large O and she nodded. Now it made perfect sense to her.

Letitia made sure Myrna headed for her bungalow before she made her way into the house. Tyler followed Myrna, turning off in the direction of the bunkhouse.

She left her clothing where she dropped it and crawled into bed. She was asleep the moment her head met the pillow. Except there was a broad smile on her face as Tyler dominated her dreams.

"YOU NEED TO USE your wrist more," Tyler advised, standing behind Letitia.

She held the coiled rope between her hands. "Why am I doing this?"

"Because you wanted to learn everything you could about ranching. Roping is part of ranching," he reminded her, standing until he was directly behind her. He put his arms in front of her and covered her hands with his. He drew the rope out into a good-sized loop and demonstrated throwing the loop over a fence post. It settled neatly around it and dropped to the ground. He stepped back and held up his hands. "See, it's easy."

Letitia daintily clapped, her gloved hands muffling the sound. "That's one fence post that isn't going to leave the herd again."

He flicked the tip of her nose. "It's easier to practice on something that won't run away from you, smart ass. Now you try it."

Letitia held the rope, slowly opened a sizable loop, stared at the post and swung her arm. At what she hoped was the right time, she flung her arm out. The loop fell woefully short of the post.

"Give me something live to practice on and I'd have a better chance," she argued.

"You drop that loop over the post and I will," he readily promised. "I doubt you'd like to be dragged across the yard by the dog."

Letitia looked over at Duffy who lay snoozing by the barn door while Le Chat sat behind him, batting at his tail with his paw. Luckily, the cat kept his claws sheathed. "Yes, I can see he'd knock me right off my feet," she said dryly. "Why don't I just drop this loop over him?"

He pointed the other way then crossed his arms in front of his chest.

"Slave driver," she muttered. She tried again, throwing the rope the short distance to the post. She missed.

"You keep working on flicking your wrist the right way and you'll get the hang of it in no time," Tyler advised as he walked off. "I'll be back to check on your progress later."

"Where do you think you're going?" She watched him go into the barn and later walk back outside leading his horse.

"I've got work to do, boss lady." He grinned as he swung into the saddle. He straightened up, gathering the reins between his gloved hands. "You know what, I just bet by the time I get back you'll have the wrist action down pat and be good enough to throw a perfect loop over that post. Have fun," he called over his shoulder as he clicked to his horse and rode out.

"I'll show him," she gritted, spinning back around. Her fury gave her strength she didn't know she had. "I'll show that cowboy I can rope this stupid post. Then I'm going to rope his dog." Two hours later, her hands were sore, her arm muscles aching and she hadn't come close to the fence post once. Bored with the show, Duffy had already roused himself from his nap and wandered off in search of more invigorating entertainment. Le Chat followed with a gleam in his eye that meant the dog was going to suffer for some unknown infraction. Jokes circulated around the ranch that the arrogant cat seemed to live for the times he could torment the large dog who, for some obscure reason, didn't fight back.

"That's right, abandon me too," she accused the dog. "You're as bad as your owner. If I didn't love him so much, I'd shoot him." She thought about her words and quickly revised them. "I may shoot him anyway."

Chapter Fourteen

"Repairing fences isn't as easy as it looks," Letitia commented, rubbing her itchy nose with her sleeve. She'd already sneezed a couple of times. "Do you think I'm allergic to the grass?" She didn't bother to wait for an answer. "Wouldn't that be something? A rancher allergic to grass. I'd probably be laughed out of the county."

"You wouldn't be the first one with the problem. Knew a guy who was allergic to hay. He took shots three times a week just so he could walk inside his barn. Hold this tighter," Tyler said absently.

She thought a change of conversation was in order. "You promised to give me another roping lesson. Don't forget."

"I won't." Using his teeth, Tyler tugged off his glove, so he could get a better grip with his bare hands.

To be honest, Letitia had woken up that morning feeling incredibly lazy and thought of doing nothing all that important.

"Leonard the attorney, called last night. He told me a few more pieces of my jewelry have been sold and the money was deposited in my bank account."

Tyler's smile was the kind she lived for. "That's great, hon. Here, hold these for me." He handed her a pair of wire cutters.

Letitia watched him wrap the top fence wire around the post and attach it with a heavy-duty staple gun.

"I guess I should thank Stephano for always salving his conscience with custom-made jewelry fashioned by an internationally known jewelry designer," she mused out loud. "I can't believe how much the designer's name alone has sent the value of those pieces upward." She slapped the cutters against Tyler's palm with the aplomb of an operating-room nurse. "It's just too bad he hadn't felt guilty more often. I might have come up with enough to pay off all the ranch's debts."

"Hold this one tighter," he ordered in an a sharp voice, crouching down.

Letitia complied, looking down at the top of his head shielded by his hat. She wiggled her nose as a drop of perspiration trickled down until it reached the tip. She started staring at her nose, fascinated by the drop.

"Stop it."

"Stop what?"

"Stop staring at that drop of sweat. You're cross-eyed. I need those pliers over there." Tyler pointed to the small cache of tools he'd earlier lined up on the blanket they'd used to sit on while they ate lunch.

She picked up the pliers he pointed to and handed them over to him.

"You enjoy doing this, don't you?"

He looked up. "Repairing fence?"

She nodded. "Not just repairing the fence, but everything you do. You don't seem to care that you're the boss and the boss is supposed to delegate. You enjoy working out here with the men, whether it's vaccinating the cattle, which I noticed was a very dirty and smelly job, or staying up all night with a sick horse."

"A boss can't do his job right unless he can do what he wants his men to do. He has to be willing to shoulder his share of the work load." He swore under his breath when a wire pricked his thumb.

Letitia stood back and admired the play of Tyler's back muscles as he made sure the fence post was still securely set in the ground. She resisted the urge to pick his shirt up and tie it into knots. There was something about the man's bare chest and back that had her thinking about destroying all his shirts.

"When do I get to ride herd?" She'd been after him on the subject for the past month.

He pulled his bandanna out of his back pocket and wiped the sweat from his face before rolling it and tying it around his forehead. "Which one did you watch last night after I left?

"I don't know what you mean." She was all wide-eyed innocence.

He slowly advanced on her. "Tell."

Letitia grinned. "*City Slickers.* I couldn't go back to sleep and thought I'd watch something funny. Otherwise, I probably would have watched *Red River* again."

He shook his head. "You are certifiable."

"But cute," she pointed out.

He checked the rest of the fencing to make sure it was secure. "Well, yeah, that too."

Preferring to ignore his teasing, Letitia picked up the canteen. She took a sip of water and walked forward to offer him some. He stole a kiss before he took the canteen from her.

She kept her eyes closed in order to better savor his kiss. "Why don't we break for lunch?" she crooned.

Tyler smothered his grin. "We already did, remember? That's why I'm behind in fixing this fence. Of course, I'm just the hired help and *you* are the real boss..." His voice wandered off on a terse note.

"Is that how you really feel? That I consider you nothing more than an employee?" She looked stricken at the idea. "Tyler, I never—"

He quickly shucked his gloves and placed his fingers over her lips to shush her. "Hey, I know that," he said quietly, although there was a decided bite to his tone and she noticed the expression in his eyes said another story. It still bothered him. A lot. "Ticia—it's something that's always going to be there between us."

"Only if you put it there!"

Tyler dropped his arms and walked away. He kept his back to her as his shouting seemed angry at both her and himself. "What should I say? That I love you? That I want to make sure you love it here so much you'll never even think of leaving? That I don't have much, but I do have my skills as a rancher?" he shouted. "That I can't let you go because you mean so much to me?" He spun around and found her standing next to him. He slowly ran his thumb over her lower lip. His eyes darkened to a stormy gray. "You're playing with fire, sweetheart,'' he warned in a raw voice.

Her eyes shimmered with tears she couldn't hold back and her smile wobbled dangerously. "Yes, I know. What're you going to do about it? I mean, you just made a very important declaration. The least you can do is act on it,'' she murmured.

He pulled in a deep breath hoping it would slow down his racing heart. He should have known better. He'd just spilled his guts to the lady. Told her everything he had been thinking for quite a while but hadn't had the nerve to say. With Letitia around, it wasn't easy to keep anything to himself.

"If we weren't out here in the open . . .'' His subtle threat floated between them.

Letitia heard it more as a promise. "No convenient cabin nearby?''

He shook his head.

"What about a tent?'' She knew he didn't have one within reach, but she figured it wouldn't hurt to ask, just in case.

His head slowly swiveled from side to side.

Letitia braced her hands on her hips. "Well, what kind of cowboy are you, anyway?'' she demanded to know. "You're not prepared for any eventuality?''

"It's the Boy Scouts who're always prepared,'' he pointed out.

She glared at him, not happy that he seemed to find this more amusing than frustrating. And pleased the tension was gone from his eyes and stance. "You don't have to sound so damned reasonable! I swear if I didn't love you so much I'd shoot you where you stand!'' she shouted.

"You think I have anything to worry about?" he hooted. "Hell, you can't even come close to hitting the fence post with a rope."

She saw red by now. "You hand me a gun and I'll show you what I can do!"

"Not if I value my life!" His jaw dropped as her earlier words finally penetrated. "Did you mean it when you said you love me?"

She raised her chin. "Mebbe." Her polished boarding school accent fractured one of J.T.'s favorite words.

Tyler took his hat off and threw it up in the air in accompaniment to his rebel yell. He picked Letitia up in his arms and spun her around in a dizzying circle.

"Tyler!" Stunned by his abrupt change of mood she could only grip his shoulders and hang on for dear life. "Tyler, you're acting crazy!"

"Do you realize what you just did?" he whooped, finally slowing down.

Still in shock over his actions, she couldn't think clearly. "Besides, threatening to shoot you?"

"You also told me you loved me. If you knew how much that means to me." His eyes shone like silver glitter against his deeply tanned features. He couldn't stop touching her, whether it was caressing her cheek with the backs of his fingers or stroking her arms.

"Are you sure you haven't been out in the sun too long?" she questioned. "Besides, I assumed you already figured it out and that's why you were willing to tell me how you felt. I don't make love just with any man who asks me."

His grin was pure euphoria. "I had a pretty good idea. At least, I hoped so, but it's always nice to hear the words."

"That goes both ways, cowboy."

Tyler's mouth curved as he looked down at the woman who'd captured his heart so securely. Her nose was sunburned, her cheeks flushed with joy. She wore cotton and denim although he found an enticing amount of silk and lace underneath the durable fabrics.

"You're hard-headed, mouthy, sometimes act like the socialite of the year and you've made me nuts since day one. I knew you were trouble for me the minute I laid eyes on you. It wasn't long before I figured it was either fall in love with you or throttle you. I figured falling in love with you would be better than spending time in a jail cell." He took a deep breath. "You're my world, Letitia Jones DeMarco. I don't want to live in it without you."

Her heart melted. She stepped forward and slid her arms around his waist. "You are a horrible chauvinist at times. You infuriate me daily. You also excite me to no end. That was when I knew the only thing I could do was fall in love with you," she said softly. She pressed a kiss against his chest. His skin was hot against her lips and streaked with perspiration and dirt from his labors, but she didn't care.

He savored the light fragrance of her cologne mixed with the heat of her skin. He combed his fingers through her ponytail. "Darlin', we chose a hell of a place to get into this discussion."

"You're the one who says there isn't a cabin nearby where we can continue this." Her reply was muffled against his chest.

Tyler's body was agreeing loud and clear with that statement. "Call it a test."

She looked up. "A test of what?"

He had to think about that one. "That we're sincere with our feelings and they aren't mistaken for lust."

"I think that was supposed to be my line," she pointed out, lacing his fingers through hers and studying his hand. There were calluses on the palm and finger pads, the backs cut and scarred. A working man's hand. She doubted she'd ever seen anything more handsome. She lifted it to her lips.

Tyler had trouble swallowing the lump growing in his throat. "I guess we'll just have to wait to finish this discussion tonight," he said huskily, pulling his shirt off his saddle and shrugging it on.

Letitia helped him get his tools together. The love shimmered between them like a heat wave. Again, Letitia thought to change the subject. Abruptly.

"I read a magazine article about raising pigs since there's been an increasing market for lean pork," she commented.

Tyler's scowl was her answer. "You don't ask a self-respecting rancher to raise *pigs.*"

Letitia threw up her hands in disgust. "Don't hold it in. Please, feel free to speak your mind," she said sarcastically, piqued by his negative response. "At least I didn't mention sheep!"

"Good thing you didn't. Why not talk about raising llamas?" He put his roll of tools in his saddle bags.

"Maybe I will! You haven't given me a chance to explain even one of my ideas in detail!" she yelled.

"Yes I have and you know it."

Letitia knew Tyler still had a problem with her being the boss, but she couldn't bring that up now. Tyler wasn't listening to her and she was fed up. She crossed her arms in front of her chest.

"All right, hotshot, *you* come up with something."

"Look, you want to do something crazy? Fine, raise frogs!" he shouted so loud he startled the horses.

"Maybe I will! Then your warts can show up on the outside instead of just on the inside!"

A stone-faced Letitia gathered up the blanket and efficiently rolled it up, securing it behind her saddle. She mounted her horse with considerably more grace than she had in the past and rode off without a backward glance.

Snatches of sentences floated back through the air to Tyler's ears. Words like "mule-headed", "impossible", "stubborn jackass" were only a few, and the more polite. He knew things were getting worse when she lapsed into Italian. She seemed to do that only when her temper was really riled.

"That woman could drive a man to drink." He mounted and immediately rode off in the opposite direction.

LETITIA'S HURRICANE FORCE stormed through the kitchen, surprising Myrna who was watching her favorite soap opera while cutting up vegetables for a stew.

"I thought the two of you were staying out all day," she commented, looking up from the screen.

Letitia stopped long enough to announce, "He deserves to be shot," before heading for the rear of the house. A door slammed hard enough to send the windows rattling.

Myrna shook her head. "I wonder if things would be more peaceful if they got married," she muttered, returning to her program. "Probably not."

Letitia sat slumped in her desk chair staring at the wall. Her most recent addition was a personal computer. She spent days inputting all the ranch records. Lately, she seemed to use it more for playing computer games than adding new files to the main directory. Her forehead creased in thought as she racked her brain. All she accomplished was a nasty headache.

"I can't believe there isn't a solution out there," she murmured to herself, absently chewing on a nail.

She looked around and thought of all the changes that had gone on, not just in the house, but within herself. She didn't think twice about getting up at the crack of dawn, ate a huge breakfast and spent most mornings riding with Tyler and the men learning the nitty-gritty part of ranching. She'd discovered that horses weren't as bad as she thought they were. She learned that she could do something more constructive than house decorating or organizing social functions. And whether she liked it or not, she had to admit that Tyler had a great deal to do with it. He constantly challenged her to push herself to the limit and even allowed her to make her own mistakes.

"Why can't life be simpler?" she groaned.

"Probably because you enjoy making it so difficult." Tyler walked into the office and sat in the chair in front of her desk. He didn't say anything else. He just watched her.

"How can we admit we love each other in one breath and fight in the next?" she asked.

"Chemistry."

Letitia sighed. "I'm trying too hard, aren't I? I thought it would be so easy to come up with a solution to the ranch's problems and it hasn't turned out that way."

He shook his head. "You're just too eager to dive into a new project. There's nothing wrong with that."

"I thought watching movies and reading books would teach me ranching." She sighed, loosening her ponytail and fluffing her hair. "I've learned more doing the dirty work you and J.T. enjoy pushing my way." She shot him a wry look.

He grinned. "That's how we all learned. And an extra pair of hands is always helpful." He grimaced. "Sam gave his notice today."

Another sad fact of life. Letitia was losing men because there wasn't enough work. She'd hoped to keep a full crew on and it wasn't working out that way. "How many does that make it now?"

"Six."

"I can't blame him." She suddenly visualized herself alone here, all gray and stooped over as she walked through a decaying house and barns. She shuddered.

"Hey." Tyler leaned across the desk and took her hand. "We're going to make it."

"Are you sure?" Her smile was a bit bleak.

"Yep. You're too stubborn to give up." He grinned, squeezing her hand.

"I can't believe you're seeing that part of me as a virtue."

"I don't know if I'd use the word virtue, but I'd say it is a plus. At times," he hastily qualified.

"Too bad Holly isn't a witch and Jack isn't a warlock," she said wistfully. "I'd get them to cast a spell and make everything all right."

"No, you wouldn't." Tyler had already been told the tale of Holly's children casting a magic spell to get them a father and Jack "appearing" before them at the opportune time. Because he lived in a known haunted house, always wore black and was very mysterious about his past, the townspeople of Salem, Massachusetts were convinced he wasn't exactly of this earth. Letitia was included in their curiosity since she and Le Chat shared the same hair and eye color and the cat always wore a collar the same color as Letitia's outfit. Now, the elegant feline seemed to wear a denim collar more than anything else.

Letitia made a face. "You're right, I wouldn't, but it sounds good. I know I could go to Jack anytime for help, but he's bailed me out enough times in the past. This time, I need to do it all on my own."

He squeezed her hand as a reminder. "Except you're not alone."

She smiled. "You're right, I'm not."

"I DON'T WANT TO HAVE to sneak out of the bunkhouse and in through your window this winter," Tyler told her as they curled up in bed together after making love. He glanced at the clock and realized his time was running out before he went through his cat burglar routine.

She held her breath in expectation. "Don't tell me you're going to change your nocturnal habits until spring."

He rolled over, effectively trapping her under his body. "Not if you can give the right answer to my question."

She traced the curve of his bicep because she was leery of the look in his face. "I won't know what I'm expected to say until I hear the question."

"I'm not rich, I'm not Italian," he stated, trapping her face between his bent arms. "But I do love you."

"Yes," she whispered.

He froze. "You're sure?"

"I know if I wasn't, you'd convince me. In fact—" she trickled her fingers against his lips. "—why don't you try anyway? Just as insurance against my changing my mind."

Tyler's mouth stretched in a broad grin. "My pleasure."

She bubbled with laughter as his mouth claimed hers.

"I HEAR YOU'LL BE GETTING married soon," Ezra Beecham said when Letitia met with him.

She nodded, not caring who saw how happy she was.

"Set a date yet?"

"No. My brother is out of the country right now and I'd like to give him the happy news that he's giving me away before we settle on a date," she explained.

"Well, don't put that boy's name on the deed," the elderly banker advised on a sour note.

She was surprised by his vehemence. "Why not?"

"A lot of men will marry a woman for land and once they've got what they've wanted, the woman is left with nothing," he stated as if his words were law.

Letitia opened her mouth to argue that Tyler was the last person to do such a horrible thing, then she closed it again. She realized by looking at the man that Mr. Beecham was only saying this out of old fashioned courtesy to a bank client who happened to be a woman.

"Thank you for the advice, Mr. Beecham," she said with her best demure smile. "I will certainly think about it."

"So you're finally going to make an honest woman of her." J.T. stared at Tyler.

The foreman stared back. "You don't act surprised."

"Hell, we've been making bets on you two since that first day." J.T. chuckled.

Tyler's eyes widened with stunned surprise. "You what?"

"You may have thought the only pool around was how long she'd stay here, but there was some of us who figured the two of you just might hit it off. The sparks were there the first time we saw you two together." He squinted in thought. "I think Pete picked the closest date. I was off by more than a week. Still, it's good you're doing the right thing."

"What do you mean by that?"

J.T. smiled knowingly. "Hell, son, I told you I don't need much sleep. You quit looking out that upstairs window and the window in your room suddenly quit squeaking. I'm glad to hear you two are going to tie the knot. Maybe the fireworks between you two will settle down some.''

''Somehow I doubt that.'' Tyler chuckled. ''Letitia has a mind of her own. If anything they'll probably get worse.''

''That's one lady you'll never grow bored with.''

Tyler's body tightened with memories of the last few nights. ''That's true.''

J.T. shifted his toothpick from one side of his mouth to the other. ''She can do a lot around here, too. She isn't afraid of getting her hands dirty.''

Tyler nodded. ''Although she still can't throw a lasso worth a damn.''

His eyes twinkled with merriment. ''Something tells me that doesn't make any difference to you.''

''Not after I took her out for target practice.'' Tyler shuddered at the memory of the human silhouette targets he'd put up against bales of hay. ''She refuses to aim for the heart or head, much less the shoulder or leg.''

''Then where does she aim for?'' J.T. followed the direction of Tyler's gaze. ''Damn,'' he breathed. ''Don't let her get mad at you, boy, or you might spend your life singing soprano.''

''MYRNA, TYLER ASKED ME to marry him and I said yes,'' Letitia announced as she helped the cook with the bread making.

''You think you're telling me anything new?'' her voice wobbled with amusement.

''How did you know?''

Myrna looked up from her mixing bowl. ''It was the day you and Tyler walked in here looking all flustered and Tyler was missing all the buttons off his shirt. I doubt he could have lost them all at once.''

Letitia pounded the dough with her fist. ''Isn't anybody surprised by our news?'' she grumbled.

''Probably not in this county.''

Chapter Fifteen

"No one is surprised we're getting married! They act as if they've known this would happen all along," Letitia complained to Tyler, then punched his arm. "Tyler, did you hear me?"

He was dozing lightly to catch up on much-needed sleep on this quiet Sunday afternoon. "Had no choice with the way you're carrying on," he mumbled, rolling over.

She resisted hitting him with her pillow. Everyone else had taken Sunday off, which left her and Tyler alone on the ranch. They'd opted for a quiet afternoon curled up in bed where they enjoyed a picnic lunch and savored each other for dessert. She curved her body around his, relishing the feel of him.

"Do you think we'll turn into a boring staid couple after the wedding?" she asked.

"No way." He rolled over to face her. "Staid and boring aren't in your vocabulary. There is something I want to talk to you about, though."

She looked up expectantly. "Sounds serious."

"I have some savings put aside and I'd like to use it to buy into the ranch, if you're willing. I'm not even talking about half," he explained. "I don't want any-one or you, especially, to think I'm along for a free ride."

"That's the last thing I'd think." She stroked his chest, tangling her fingers in the curling hair. "We can draw up papers, do it anyway you'd like. Although you may be putting your money down a dry hole."

"Nah, we'll get there. You'll see."

Her hands dipped downward. "I see a lot. And feel even more."

He drew in a sharp breath. "Then I guess we better do something about it." He rubbed his hips against hers.

She almost purred with delight. "Yes, I guess we better."

After they made love, Tyler fell into a deep sleep. Letitia felt too energized to sleep. She finally crept out of bed and headed for the living room. She picked up the television's remote control and switched channels until a program snagged her attention. As Letitia remained riveted to the TV, she quickly made notes.

"This could be it," she whispered excitedly when the program finished. "He said something about this before, but I thought he was kidding."

"Ticia. *Letitia*!" Tyler's panicked shout reverberated through the house.

She jumped up and ran back to the bedroom. She skidded to a stop in the doorway because she couldn't believe what she was seeing.

"Get him off," Tyler gritted, staring at Le Chat who sat on Tyler's thighs, batting at the quilt with unsheathed claws.

She grimaced. "Hmm. This could prove dangerous."

Tyler sucked in a breath. "Ticia, if you don't do something real soon, there's a good chance we won't have any kids."

Letitia crooned to the cat, walking slowly forward so she wouldn't startle him. Instead of bounding over to his mistress, the cat batted at another quilt hill. Tyler uttered a curse. He didn't take his eyes off the cat once.

"Okay, cat, you win," he said softly. "You've turned my dog into a zombie and you've shown me who's boss. Are you happy now?"

Le Chat lazily got to his feet. He stared at Tyler for several minutes, his tail waving slowly like a warrior's banner going into battle. He walked up Tyler's body oblivious to the man's pained expression, paused long enough to scrape his rough tongue across Tyler's face then gracefully jumped off the bed. Convinced he truly was the one in charge, he sauntered out of the room.

"I guess we have to invite him to the wedding now," Tyler muttered, glaring at the cat's back.

By now, Letitia's shoulders were shaking with laughter. She walked over to the bed and collapsed on it, still trying to hold her mirth back.

"Don't," he warned. "Not one word."

She shook her head. Her lips trembled and she bit down hard. "If you could have seen it the way I did," her voice vibrated.

"Ticia, he almost castrated me. I see nothing funny in that."

She rolled over onto her stomach and buried her face in the quilt. By now her entire body was trembling with the effort she exerted in holding back her mirth.

"That cat isn't real," Tyler decided.

That was the last straw. She began howling, but Tyler still didn't see anything funny in it.

"I'm going to have a long talk with my dog," he muttered.

Once Letitia calmed down, she recalled what she'd just seen and ran back to the living room with her notepad.

"A couple of weeks ago, when we fought you said something about llamas," she told him, holding out the pad. "There was a program on television about the rise in llama breeders."

Tyler sat up and looked over her notes.

"They graze on pasture grass," she told him excitedly. "And alfalfa and grass hay. The deep snows aren't any problem since they originate in the Himalayas." She snuggled down next to him, looking over his shoulder.

"I remember meeting some man from Oregon who raised them," he mused. "They're being used more and more for wilderness packing and transporting up mountains instead of mules. And as pets." He looked up. "I also remember him saying they're not cheap. They've become so popular their worth has almost skyrocketed. That usually means an adult female is not easy to find and buy," he warned. "And as with any livestock breeding, you don't see a profit right off."

"If Running Springs has survived this long, there's no reason we can't keep it running for the time needed to get the operation up and running. And we could sell off the last of the cattle," she pointed out. "And we look for young females if we can't get any adults. Gestation period is eleven and a half months and the female can be bred again two weeks after delivery. In fact, they're pregnant most of the time, which would give us an edge, wouldn't it?"

Tyler's lips twitched. "Sounds good to me."

Letitia glared at him. "I'm serious!"

"So am I." He leaned over and kissed her to show just how serious he was. "I might still have that breeder's business card. I'll look for it and give him a call. I also heard there's a breeder over in Columbia Falls. I'll make some calls."

Letitia threw herself into his arms. "This could be it, Tyler!" She laughed with excitement. "Out of that argument came the germ of an idea!"

He shook his head in wonderment. "I thought I was making a joke but I guess I wasn't."

She was caught up already. "Let's start checking all this out now." She started to get up.

Tyler grasped her arm and slowly pulled her back toward him. "I think it can wait a little while," he murmured, nuzzling the soft skin in the curve of her shoulder.

"You're right," she breathed, melting against him. "It can wait."

FOR THE NEXT FEW WEEKS, Letitia and Tyler made a lot of phone calls and traveled to llama ranches where they spoke to breeders, observed the calm animals and made a lot of calculations.

"We still don't have enough money," Tyler told her.

"But we have a lot of information on paper, right?" she asked, holding up a computer disk that they'd added information to on almost a daily basis. "And it proves this is a good investment and a potential money-maker."

He nodded, then broke into a slow grin as what she said fell into place. "Good old Mr. Beecham. He'll probably have a stroke when we lay this out before him."

"Maybe not. He'll feel he has us under his thumb again. That just might make his day." Letitia walked around the chair and settled down on Tyler's lap. "I was wondering what you'd think about letting the men have a say. After all, they know what we've been doing, but we really haven't talked about it at length."

"They'd adore you even more," he said quietly.

AFTER THE EVENING MEAL, Letitia asked everyone to remain for a few minutes.

"As you all know, Tyler and I have been looking into alternatives for running cattle," she announced right off. "It appears we have a good bet by breeding llamas and with luck, we can work into it on a large scale."

"Llamas?" J.T. looked confused. "You mean those long-necked animals from South America?"

She nodded. "They've become very popular as pets, watch animals and pack animals. They have good temperaments and their worth is increasing all the time." She proceeded to lay out the facts and figures in front of them by providing each man with a sheet of paper.

"Why are you talking to all of us about this?" Ben asked, looking at her with a confused frown.

"Because you men have been very loyal in staying through the hard times and we hope you'll stay with us during the good. If this works the way I hope it will, it will be your future too," she said simply. "They've proved to be more than a fad pet and we could even sell that upper pasture since we wouldn't need all the land. Right now, we have the available funds to buy four animals. I talked to one breeder who's willing to sell us a pregnant female. And naturally, extremely cold climates don't bother them. That's a big plus. Tyler and I talked to Mr. Beecham about refinancing the existing loan, and while he grew a little red in the face and choked a lot, he is seriously considering our proposal." The men chuckled at that.

"We'd have our own cashmere yarn right here for knitting," Myrna pronounced.

"Do we want to devote everything to the llamas?" J.T. asked.

"It looks good," Tyler answered. "It won't be like running cattle or horses."

The couple nodded.

They waited tensely for the men's response.

"Think llamas are easier to herd than cattle?" one man asked.

"Hell, anything's got to be easier than cattle," another replied with a laugh.

"Llama roundups."

"Git along little llamas!"

Tyler's eyes met Letitia's across the length of the table. "I think they agree."

Letitia smiled broadly and launched herself into Tyler's arms. The men quickly dispersed. "Think you'd mind receiving two pair of llamas for a wedding present?" she asked.

He grinned, allowing all his love for her to show. "Mind? How many men get a wedding present like that? You better hope your brother is home, because I don't intend to wait any longer," he told her. "We've got a lot of work ahead of us, darlin'."

She licked her lips. "I think we've waited long enough. I'll call him right away." She quashed any guilt at the thought of getting married without Jack present.

"It's not going to be easy," Tyler quietly warned her. "We're both stubborn to the core."

Her smile lit up the room. "Yes, but we each have our ways of persuading the other to see our side, don't we?" She idly fiddled with his shirt button before releasing it and sliding her fingers inside.

"That we do." He'd take his revenge later when he was assured they wouldn't be disturbed.

Letitia was lucky. Jack was home. And like all the others, not surprised at her news. A date was immediately set and Letitia could expect her family to arrive within the week. Holly told her she would take care of the wedding dress and accessories.

"It is not fair that not one person was surprised we're getting married," she groused to Tyler as she curled up in his arms.

"I wouldn't worry." He nuzzled the tender spot just behind her ear. "You give me more than enough surprises to make up for it."

"Then I'll do my best to keep up the tradition," she vowed, wiggling just enough to get the reaction she wanted.

Epilogue

Four Years Later

Tyler looked out over the pasture dotted with llamas varying in color from a pure creamy white to a pale tan. The two pair they started out with increased beyond their expectations and with the refinanced loan they were able to expand. It wasn't long before the demand for Running Springs llamas had increased right along with it.

"Ticia's family arrives today, don't they?" J.T. asked.

He nodded. "They're stopping by on their way to New Mexico where Jack plans to do some research for his next book. Letitia has been running around all morning making sure everything is all right." He grimaced. "She's supposed to rest, but does she listen to me?"

"Has she ever?"

"True," he ruefully admitted. "But I can hope."

"Ever think the operation would get this big?" J.T. chuckled as one snow white llama made her soft humming and clicking sounds as she approached. He stroked her muzzle and murmured to her. "Yes, darlin', you are the prettiest one here."

Tyler shook his head at the older man's affection for the animal. "Nor did I expect celebrities would be coming to us. She was a stubborn lady about this when it started, but it worked out." He turned when he saw a black sedan head up the road. "Looks like they're here." He walked around to the front of the house where he found his wife hurrying out the door. "Hey, countess, no running!" he warned.

She wrinkled her nose as she slowed her pace. "I was not running. I was walking fast. The doctor believes in exercise."

"Yeah, well, he isn't the one watching you do things you're not supposed to." As her pregnancy progressed he found that he couldn't stop looking at her and feeling the changes taking place in her body. They both oohed and ahhed over the child making his or her presence known to the prospective parents.

In a little over two months, there would be an addition to the Barnes family. He wasn't sure who was more excited about the upcoming baby: him, Letitia or the men. With everyone watching out for her, she wasn't allowed to lift anything heavier than a feather. He stood behind her and slid his arms around where her waist used to be.

"I look like Humpty Dumpty."

"Yeah, but you're *my* Humpty Dumpty," he reminded her, playfully bumping his hips against hers.

The car slowed to a stop and doors immediately opened with a nine-year-old boy hopping out followed by an eleven-year-old girl.

"Aunt Ticia!" Caro squealed, running toward Letita.

"Hey, do I get to play with the llamas?" Ryan asked without further ado. "I wanted to bring Toby, but Mom said he was too big to bring on the plane. He could have fit in one of the seats!"

"Slow down," Holly scolded them as she climbed out of the car and reached in the back seat to release the occupant of a child seat. The ten-month-old boy had his father's hair and eyes, and most especially a devilish smile that warmed his mother's heart. Five years of marriage to Jack had changed Holly into a self-confident woman who firmly believed she could take on the world. She rolled her eyes at her son's remark. "Right, just what we need is that crazy Labrador running all over. I swear that dog is bigger than Ryan!"

But it was the man Letitia's eager eyes lingered on. Tall, black-haired with now a touch of silver at the temples that only increased speculation about his rumored magical powers, Jack Montgomery headed for his sister. As Tyler released her, Jack took her hands and held them out at her sides. Dressed in a bright turquoise tunic top and black leggings, she didn't look like a married woman of four years and in her last trimester of pregnancy.

"I'd say ranch life agrees with you, sister dear," he said quietly as he pulled her into his arms for a hug.

Letitia hugged him just as tightly before looking over her shoulder. "It's more like the *man* agrees with me. Luck is on our side."

"Where Ticia is concerned, I wouldn't exactly use the word agrees," Tyler said dryly, thinking of their argument just the other day over what color to paint the nursery. He'd since come to the conclusion they only fought because they enjoyed making up so much.

Jack grinned as he understood what Tyler was talking about. "Luck has nothing to do with it, Ticia. It was all magic, remember?"

She snuggled against Tyler's chest as he came forward to reclaim his wife and put out his hand to greet Jack. "Then I'd call it magic of the best kind."

Relive the romance...
Harlequin and Silhouette
are proud to present

by Request

A program of collections of three complete novels by the most requested authors with the most requested themes. Be sure to look for one volume each month with three complete novels by top name authors.

In June: **NINE MONTHS** Penny Jordan
Stella Cameron
Janice Kaiser

Three women pregnant and alone. But a lot can happen in nine months!

In July: **DADDY'S HOME** Kristin James
Naomi Horton
Mary Lynn Baxter

Daddy's Home... and his presence is long overdue!

In August: **FORGOTTEN PAST** Barbara Kaye
Pamela Browning
Nancy Martin

Do you dare to create a future if you've forgotten the past?

Available at your favorite retail outlet.

HE HAD TO BE REAL

Did ghosts have silky hair and piercing eyes? Were their bodies lean and hard? Emily Morrell didn't think so. But Captain Calvert T. Witherspoon, late of His Majesty's service, *was* walking through walls. Emily heard the rumors about Henderson House being haunted, but she didn't know her intoxicating fantasy ghost was more man than she could handle.

CHARLOTTE MACLAY brings you a delightful tale this month, about a ghost with a very special touch...

#488 A GHOSTLY AFFAIR
by Charlotte Maclay
On sale now!

When a man loves a woman, there's nothing he wouldn't do for her....

For a close encounter of the most sensual kind, don't miss American Romance #488 A GHOSTLY AFFAIR.

HGH1

**Harlequin is proud to present our
best authors and their best books.
Always the best for your reading
pleasure!**

Throughout 1993, Harlequin will bring you
exciting books by some of the top names in
contemporary romance!

In June,
look for
*Threats and
Promises* by

BARBARA
DELINSKY

The plan was to make her nervous....

Lauren Stevens was so preoccupied with her new looks
and her new business that she really didn't notice a
pattern to the peculiar "little incidents"—incidents
that could eventually take her life. However, she did
notice the sudden appearance of the attractive and
interesting Matt Kruger who *claimed* to be a close
friend of her dead brother....

**Find out more in THREATS AND
PROMISES . . . available wherever Harlequin
books are sold.**

MEN MADE IN AMERICA

Fifty red-blooded, white-hot, true-blue hunks from every
State in the Union!

Beginning in May, look for MEN MADE IN AMERICA!
Written by some of our most popular authors, these
stories feature fifty of the strongest, sexiest men, each
from a different state in the union!

Two titles available every other month at your favorite
retail outlet.

In May, look for:

FULL HOUSE by Jackie Weger (Alabama)
BORROWED DREAMS by Debbie Macomber (Alaska)

In July, look for:

CALL IT DESTINY by Jayne Ann Krentz (Arizona)
ANOTHER KIND OF LOVE by Mary Lynn Baxter
(Arkansas)

You won't be able to resist MEN MADE IN AMERICA!